Caryl Lewis

Seed

Illustrated by
George Ermos

MACMILLAN CHILDREN'S BOOKS

Published 2022 by Macmillan Children's Books
an imprint of Pan Macmillan
The Smithson, 6 Briset Street, London EC1M 5NR
EU representative: Macmillan Publishers Ireland Ltd, 1st Floor,
The Liffey Trust Centre, 117–126 Sheriff Street Upper
Dublin 1, D01 YC43
Associated companies throughout the world
www.panmacmillan.com

ISBN 978-1-5290-7766-7

Text copyright © Caryl Lewis 2022
Illustrations copyright © George Ermos 2022

The right of Caryl Lewis and George Ermos to be identified as
the author and illustrator of this work has been asserted by them
in accordance with the Copyright, Designs and Patents Act 1988.

1 3 5 7 9 8 6 4 2

A CIP catalogue record for this book is available from the British Library.

Printed and bound by CPI Group (UK) Ltd, Croydon CR0 4YY

For my husband Aled, and our children
Hedd, Gwenno and Guto.
Love and imagination are all you need.

CHAPTER ONE

This is a list of what Marty's grandad had:

1 pair of spectacles (one arm broken)
7 teeth
1 single-room bedsit above the
    Crown and Anchor public house
1 broken outboard engine
457 teabags
1 tub of powdered milk
A lot of time
1 allotment with shed (with a giant map
    of the world nailed to the wall inside)
1 squeaky camping chair that tried to
    swallow you whole if you sat on it funny
Very sparkly blue eyes
1 old trilby hat
1 Hodgkins & Taylor & Sons seed catalogue
1 empty biscuit tin

This may sound like a lot, but it kind of isn't. Not compared to Marty's mum. Marty's mum had billions of things. Billions and trillions and infinity of them. I mean I'd make a list, but even if you lived to be a hundred I don't think that you'd ever finish reading it because Marty's mum kept everything. Newspapers and holey shoes and rusty lawnmowers and unread books and broken picture frames and, well, EVERYTHING. When she used to be able to leave the house, she could never pass a skip on the side of the road without reaching in and bringing something 'useful' home, and she got really stamp-footed and scared if you tried to throw anything away.

Marty's house was the one at the end of the road with the overgrown garden with all the stuff in it. There were washing machines that didn't work and piles of carpet rolled up like soggy cigars. There were coils of cables and old sofas stacked on top of each other. The house wasn't very big to begin with, a bungalow with four small rooms and a sort of narrow kitchen and a square room out the back, but ever since Marty was born the house had been shrinking. Not actually shrinking, like magically shrinking, but it was definitely getting smaller.

He didn't actually remember ever having been into their living room. It had always been full of stuff, but he kind of remembered sneaking into his mum and dad's bedroom when he was little, when his dad was still around, and sliding into their bed for cuddles in the middle of the night. But you couldn't even open that door now as so many piles of stuff blocked the way.

After a while, the corridors had started to fill on both sides, leaving only a thin path through from the narrow kitchen to his bedroom. You could only get to one cupboard in the kitchen, and the sink, and that was always full. Mum slept at the back of the kitchen now, in a lounge chair by the back door, and the only time she went outside was when she'd sit on the back step and smoke. In the bathroom, the bath had been filled with old letters and bags of clothes so that he could only have a stand-up wash with a flannel and some soap and half a sink of semi-warm water.

So far, Marty had managed to save his bedroom. Every time a bag of stuff was put there, he'd push it out again, a bit like standing on the beach and pushing back the waves with your bare hands. So that's why he went to see

Grandad at his allotment every night after school. Even though they did nothing, really, except sit outside the garden shed and drink tea from enamel mugs together, it was a break from the squashiness of home, the sense that you were about to be washed away by a tide of stuff.

'All right, Marty boy?' Grandad flashed his toothy grin and passed him a mug of tea so sweet you could live off it for a week.

Marty sat down quietly and shrugged. Now, Grandad was always sparkly-eyed, but today he was fizzing inside about something. This wasn't entirely unusual, because Grandad had a history of getting very excited about strange things. Such as the time he thought he had brewed a new wonder-fuel from rhubarb leaves and wanted to call NASA, and the time he built an automatic slug squisher out of six pairs of old boots and an ancient Hoover, oh, and the time he built the bum scratcher 2000, and the automatic tea stirrer 250, which worked so well that it stirred and stirred Marty's mug of tea until it started sloshing from side to side more and more violently until, suddenly, it flew off sideways in a spray of scalding liquid, forcing them both to throw themselves on the ground for fear of burning themselves. Today, though, Marty could tell that something else was up.

'I got you something.' Grandad smiled. 'Been waiting for it to arrive for weeks!'

He pulled a small, brown envelope from his pocket and held it out.

'Happy birthday, Marty, my boy.'

Marty blushed. He thought everyone had forgotten. His mum hadn't said anything this morning. Even he had tried to forget for most of the day too.

'I didn't have much money but I wanted to get you something special . . .'

Marty didn't get many presents and, since the house had started filling, Marty didn't really care for 'stuff', but it was nice that Grandad had remembered.

'Open it, then,' said Grandad eagerly, his eyes prompting Marty to tear open the envelope. Even though he wasn't a kid any more, Marty still felt the shyness of being watched while opening a present.

Marty took his time. He put down his mug of tea and slid his finger under the envelope flap. It was a small, brown, square one, like the kind they used to put his mum's wages in when she worked at the shop. His grandad was still smiling at him. The envelope was so light that it didn't seem to have anything in it, to be honest. So he tipped it upside down and shook it over his palm and out plopped a seed. Marty's heart fell a little.

'Wow!' he said. 'A seed!'

'One of Hodgkins and Taylor and Sons' finest, I'll have you know!'

Grandad was smiling at him still. Marty didn't quite know what he had been expecting, but it wasn't this. He swallowed down his disappointment.

'It's really great . . .' he heard himself saying.

Marty held the seed in his fingers. It *was* an extraordinarily large seed. Smooth, with a plump belly, and it was lightly striped as if it were wearing pyjamas. Marty studied it: it was too big for a sunflower, too pippy-shaped for a flower . . .

'What kind of seed is it?'

Grandad flashed a grin of excitement.

'That, my boy, is a surprise! I could only afford one, so let's hope it's a good one!'

Marty's smile was fading.

'Listen,' Grandad said, 'I'm sorry I couldn't get you those computer games and things that the kids have these days. I'd give you the whole world if I could. You know that, don't you?'

'I know,' said Marty softly.

'And you never know what this little stunner has in store for us,' Grandad said, taking the seed from Marty's palm. 'There's magic in seeds, you know.' He winked.

'You can never tell what wonders are in them.'

Marty looked at his grandad with his usual mix of love and confusion.

'It is a lovely seed,' he said.

Grandad held it up to the last light of day and studied it, his whole body quivering with excitement.

'You're right, my boy – it's a beauty! It's a rollicking beauty!'

CHAPTER TWO

This is a list of what Marty had:

1 old BMX bike
2 jumpers that fitted him: one red, one blue
As many books as he could pull from the stuff in
the house
1 mother who wouldn't leave the house
1 five-centimetre-tall statue of the Eiffel Tower
given to him when he was tiny by the dad he
hadn't seen since he was four, which he kept in
his pocket
1 uniform donated to him by the school, which
included:
1 pair of trousers with the name Harry Thomas
sewn inside them
1 school T-shirt with the name Nathan Sharp
written in ink on the collar

1 school jumper with Lee Smith written on the
    washing instruction label (Marty didn't mind
    not having his own school uniform, except that
    when he lost an item of clothing at breaktime or
    after PE, he'd have to remember four names –
    his own and all of these others – in order to get
    his stuff back)
Half a packet of toffee chews
A single bed with a Mickey Mouse duvet cover he
    was way too old for

'I'm home!' Marty shouted, but his voice was kind of
snuffed out.

That was the thing with their home. There was so
much clutter inside that it seemed to dim any noise. It
squished you into quietness and stillness. Marty closed
the front door behind him. He'd been to the shop to
pick up the dinner and some milk, and had hung the
thin, plastic bag on the handlebars of his BMX as he
rode home. They usually had pie because you could
bake it in its own tin, and Marty had found that if you
swished it out with water afterwards, and added it to the
pile of old pie tins, then they slipped into each other,

taking up not very much room.

'You taken your tablets?' he shouted.

'Yes!' came back the muffled voice. Marty could hear his mum dragging stuff about.

'What are you doing?' shouted Marty.

'You'll see!'

Mum would sleep a lot, and still be really tired, so it was weird to hear her moving about so much. Marty set about opening the pie lid with a tin opener and pushed some dirty dishes aside in order to jam the kettle under the tap to run some water to make some tea for his mum.

Marty fished out two dirty plates from the sink and ran them under the tap. He set the oven timer for twenty minutes.

When he stepped into the back room, he almost couldn't believe his eyes. His mum had cleared a corner of the room. She stood there, hot and sweaty in a baggy T-shirt, her hair tied in a knot at the top of her head, determination in her eyes. She'd put some papers into a bag. She'd found some rubbish bags and had filled at least two. She was out of breath.

'I can do this,' she said, a proud smile on her face.

Marty's heart sank. *Not again*, he thought.

'I've almost cleared in here.'

Marty looked around and, yes, there was a small, clear space, but everything else was exactly as it had been. His mum did this every now and again. It was as if she came alive for a little bit. It was as if she woke up and looked around and thought, *This is crazy*, and started to clear. And she would. And sometimes it would last a day, and sometimes it would last a week, but usually no longer than that. After a while, it was as if the fog would come back, her body would slow down and slowly but surely all the mess would come back, sometimes worse than before.

'What do you think?' his mum asked, grinning.

'It's great,' Marty lied.

'It is, isn't it?' she said again, looking around, hands on hips. 'I'm going to get it sorted this time . . .'

Marty felt a tightening in his stomach.

'Of course you are,' he said, not for the first time. 'Anyway, the dinner's on.'

His mum nodded.

'I'll give you a shout when it's ready.'

'OK!' she said, getting back to her cleaning, her eyes shining.

Marty went to check on the pie. He used to get really upset by the whole thing. The embarrassment, the frustration, the wanting her to just be normal. Just a normal, boring, nag-you-to-tidy-your-room kind of mum. But weirdly, over the years, he had also made a kind of room in his head. And he'd stuffed all the 'Sorry, you can't come back to mine – my mum's not home' and the 'Sorry, sir, I forgot my new book at the library' and the 'Yeah, we went away over the summer too' excuses into it. He'd pushed them in and squished the door shut, and had become really good at not thinking too much about any of it.

Grandad had tried helping her years ago. He'd come over with a few of his friends. They'd hired a skip, a big yellow bucket thing, and got a lorry-crane-ma-jiggy to drop it into the garden. They'd opened the back door and started to carry stuff out. Mum had followed them around all day, wringing her hands and saying, 'Not that! Not that!' and, 'I'll find a use for that; that'll come in handy.' Marty kind of understood her wanting to keep books and things like that, but who on earth would find a use for six broken radiators or a stack of mismatched window frames? He remembered her and Grandad shouting at each other. Louder and louder until all Grandad's friends went to sit in their van. That was the last time they'd talked to each other. Grandad hadn't been at the house since and he barely asked about Mum any more.

The timer rang. Marty fished out the pie with a fork on to two plates and turned sideways to walk down the back corridor where his mum was now sitting, exhausted, in her old armchair. Marty passed her her plate. She blew out her cheeks . . .

'Gosh, what would I do without you? Eh?'

Marty shrugged, sitting on the pile of newspapers he usually sat on.

'You really are an angel.'

Marty watched her as she started to eat, and his smile slowly straightened.

CHAPTER THREE

It was always the ones with new trainers that started it. Being the top predators at school, they seemed to have super-vision or something. They could sense kids like Marty scurrying around in the undergrowth and they'd pounce on them when they least expected it. In the dinner queue, 'Oi, stinkfest!' At break, 'It's Stig of the Dump!' And as Marty unchained his BMX from the railings before cycling to the allotments, 'Heh heh! Does that thing even work? You'd be quicker walking, mate!'

Teachers told Marty to ignore them. Mr Garraway, the school counsellor, had told him not to 'engage'. His mother told him to walk away, but it was his grandad who had given him the best advice. He had taught him to call them names under his breath. Awful, skin-crawling,

16

cheek-reddening, naughty, rude, horrible names. Words that you should NEVER say aloud. Words that would get you in a LOT of trouble. But, funnily enough, it kind of worked. A bit like holding your hand in ice-cold water, you could stand stuff for longer if you just let rip in your head. Like he was doing now.

'You shouldn't use words like that you know.'

Marty almost jumped out of his skin.

'Jeepers!' he cried. 'Sneak up on someone, why don't you?'

The girl smiled. Marty rattled the padlock off his bike at last.

'That needs some oil,' she said.

She was right. She stood there smiling at him and suddenly Marty found her extremely and unusually irritating.

'How'd you know what I was saying anyway?' he asked.

'I can lip-read.'

'What? You got some kind of superpower, or what?' he said impatiently.

'Well, if you call being deaf a superpower, then yup.'

Marty's irritation melted into regret.

'Oh,' he mumbled. 'I'm sorry.'

'Sorry for what?' she asked. 'That I'm deaf? Or that you have the social skills of a baked bean?'

Marty laughed out loud. She smiled, then she looked at him more sternly.

'You shouldn't let them talk to you like that you know.'

Marty shrugged.

'I'm Gracie . . .' she said.

'I'm Marty . . .' he answered.

Marty had noticed her before. She'd started school a couple of months ago, and like all the new kids had been surrounded by curious potential friends for a day or two before being brutally dropped once the novelty wore off. Although she was in the same year as Marty, she was in a different class, so they didn't come across each other very often. Looking at her now, she was kind of one of those looks-like-everyone-else people. Brown hair. A few freckles. Not big. Not small. Not tall. Not short. Kind of in-the-middle normalness. The only thing extraordinary about her, which he'd never noticed until now, was what looked like a hearing aid in her ear

18

and a button-shaped thingy in her hair.

Gracie interrupted his thoughts. 'And you shouldn't stare either.'

'Oh, no. I wasn't.'

'Yes, you were. You're a terrible liar. Gosh, you really are a disaster, aren't you?'

She was still smiling at him. He went back to being annoyed at her.

'Anyway, listen, I've got to go,' he said, turning his bike round. He usually felt as if his head was too large for his narrow shoulders and that his clothes were two sizes too big for him and that his hair, which he cut himself in the bathroom mirror, was wonky, but standing in front of her was making all of this worse. 'I'll see you later,' he said as he turned away.

'Maybe,' she said. 'Enjoy yourself at the allotments.'

'Hang on. How do you know about . . . ?' He turned back to ask, but she was already walking away.

The stink reached Marty half a mile away from the allotments. His cheeks flushed and he knew instantly what was up. Every year, in early spring, Grandad would call by the back of the fishmongers on the Old Barley Road and pick up a bucket full of the stinkiest, smelliest, disgustingest fish innards and bones and heads that they had. The more putrid and stomach-churningly puke-festy, the better. He'd smile and carry this bucket of gloop all the way back through town, waving a cheery 'good morning' to everyone as he walked by, and then he'd giggle as he heard them gagging behind him. Then, when he arrived at the allotments, he'd splatter it liberally about so that it released a stench that made the birds in the nearby trees faint, making all the neighbours turn green and call him names.

'Where've you been, Marty boy? You're late! You're late! Come and look! Come and look!'

Marty pushed the gate open.

'Yeah. I think I can guess what you've been doing, Grandad.'

'Everything's had a good thorough soaking in it!' his grandad said with his usual gappy-toothed grin.

After he'd spread the grey, pukey mixture everywhere, he would then bottle up what was left, swearing it was the best soil tonic in the world.

The city centre itself had once been rich, the size of the houses and banks in the middle of town told you that, but now it seemed to be shrivelling. Factories had shut and the big houses chopped and changed into tiny flats. Shops were closing on the high street and the only big houses left were the three-storey-high ones that ran in a ridge along the side of the allotments.

Grandad's allotment was around nine metres by three metres. Not very big, but Marty was always astounded by how much food Grandad could grow. He would sow potatoes and runner beans and courgettes and squashes. He'd always have peas and carrots, of course, and onions and beetroot. He'd swap vegetable seeds with John Trinidad, his Caribbean neighbour on the allotments, and have salads and root vegetables that he didn't even know the name of. Sadiq, three allotments down, would give him seeds of herbs and greens so leafy they looked tropical and for chilies so hot they'd blow your head off. Colin, whose day job was being a milkman, would potter around growing the most beautiful dahlias you've ever seen.

It was like a little town on the edge of the city, really,

where you could put your name down for a little patch of land the council didn't know what to do with, and, even though everyone spoke different languages and looked different and grew different things, they all had two things in common: 1) they were all skint and were happy to grow some extra food; and 2) none of them had lost that joy of watching something they'd planted grow.

Marty would laugh at the way they all helped each other but also kept back secret tricks and methods, which they would NEVER share with each other. There seemed to be what Grandad would call a 'healthy competition' about the whole thing.

Everything Grandad needed to work the soil was stored in the garden shed. Tools (old and borrowed), some envelopes to store seed, wooden crates to overwinter vegetables and a big book in which Grandad would write what had been planted every year and where. If you planted things in the same place year after year, then diseases and pests would build up in the soil and ruin whatever you planted, so Grandad was always moving things around like a massive elaborate board game. Sometimes, if the fish tonic didn't work, then he'd sprinkle the soil with ashes from the fire, and if that didn't work he'd make a brew from stinging nettles. These he would leave (along with a few secret ingredients) in a bucket of water to rot for weeks and weeks and weeks in order to make a stinky, slimy, green-black liquid that was perfect for growing big juicy vegetables.

So now, in late April, the allotment looked empty, the seed beds and soil were totally bare, but there was still a lot of preparatory work and planning to do. Grandad always said that this was the time to put in the work in order to get the rewards later on, even if, on the surface of things, nothing much would seem to be happening.

Today, he had been busy clearing a space for Marty's seed and was bouncing up and down, seemingly impervious to the vile stink that clung to everything.

'It's getting the best bed in the house,' Grandad said proudly.

All day Grandad had weeded, hoed and raked, and, to be fair, the seed bed looked good enough to sleep in. Then he brought out his enamel mug. In it was the seed. Soaking in water.

'You drowning it?' asked Marty.

Grandad smiled. 'I'm waking it up.'

He then scooped out the slimy seed and slipped it into Marty's hands.

'You do it.' He grinned as if he were about to witness a magical spectacle, and his eyes widened like a small child's in the front row of a circus.

'Me?'

'Yes! It's yours. Pointy end down.'

'How deep down?' asked Marty.

'Five centimetres,' Grandad said.

Marty approached the seed bed.

'In the middle! Give it plenty of room to grow!'

Marty held the seed a moment, its belly fat in his fingers. Then he knelt, picked a spot and slowly pushed it, pointy end down, into the crumbly soil. As his nose got closer to the earth, he detected wafts of fish and nettle and goodness knows what. Grandad was watching him, spellbound. Marty watched as the seed disappeared into the dark soil, but as his fingers pushed it down something extraordinary happened. He was sure, for a split second, that he saw it glow a brilliant white. His fingers felt a sudden flash of heat that plucked through his hand and

then his arm like an electric shock. He snatched his hand back sharply.

'What's wrong?' Grandad asked.

Marty jumped to his feet, his heart beating.

'Marty?'

Marty shook his head. It was so ridiculous. He took his fingers in his other hand. He must have imagined it. He looked up at his grandad.

'N-n-nothing,' he stuttered. 'Nothing . . .'

'OK,' Grandad said, clapping his old hands. 'Now

tuck it in, say goodnight! Shall we sing it a lullaby?'

'No!' Marty smiled distractedly, gently patting some raked soil over the seed.

Grandad slapped him on the shoulder and beamed. 'You and me are going to have so much fun!' he said, before going into the shed to boil the kettle.

Marty brushed the soil off his fingers on the side of his trousers, his fingers still tingling from the touch of the seed.

CHAPTER FOUR

Marty had been dreaming about the seed when he heard the noises in the night. To be honest, though, it was quite normal in Marty's house to hear landslides at three o'clock in the morning. It didn't take much: maybe a breeze from a window left ajar or a lorry vibrating past on the road outside was enough to send a pile of paper or boxes sliding away. Mum always tried to stack things carefully and safely – it was just that now and again something would give and then it was a bit like those videos you see of dominoes. One pile would hit another and suddenly half a room of contents would shift sideways. Marty would wake up sometimes in a cold sweat, dreaming that he was suffocating under a mound of things.

This morning, he'd got up, pulled on his trousers (he always slept in his school T-shirt and socks and pants) and made his way through the narrow corridor to the back of the kitchen.

Marty couldn't actually believe it. The whole room had been cleared. The whole of the back room. The carpet was in a right state – dirt and stains everywhere – but other than that, there was nothing in there. Only his mum, and her chair. And their old record player. She had never managed this before. All the stuff had been bagged and stacked outside the back door, so high that it touched the eves of the bungalow. She'd even spread a little blanket on the floor and had laid out a kind of breakfast picnic. If you could call it that – a few packets of crisps and some squash.

'Happy birthday, Marty!' she cried.

Marty thought for a moment if he should tell her his birthday had been and gone, but he decided to go with it.

'Thanks, Mum!'

'What do you think?!'

'I . . . I . . . I don't know what to say . . .' confessed Marty. 'I mean, did you stay up all night?'

'Almost,' she said. 'I'm having a good old spring clean! Come on, sit down . . .' She patted the floor by her side.

Marty sat down hesitantly.

'Tuck in . . .' She chucked a packet of crisps at him and opened one for herself.

'It feels really weird, doesn't it?' she said, munching the crisps.

It did feel weird. And huge. The room seemed absolutely massive. It wasn't, of course, but it just seemed that way, having been so full of stuff.

'Listen, there's even a bit of an echo . . . MRS PRITCHARD NEXT DOOR IS A PAIN IN THE BUM!' she shouted at the top of her voice.

Marty laughed. 'Mum!' But she was right. It was kind of echo-y. 'Mrs Pritchard is OK . . .'

'No, she's not,' said Mum. 'She complains to the council about me all the time.'

Then she looked terribly guilty and Marty's heart sank as he wondered what all this had been leading up to. She shifted her weight from one bum cheek to the other and pulled out another letter from her back jean pocket.

'Please don't be mad . . .' she said. That was never a good

start, thought Marty. 'I meant to show you last week.'

Marty took the letter; it was squished and folded over. He smoothed it out on his thigh.

'They're . . . they're sending a public health officer out.'

Marty's shoulders dropped. He kind of knew there must be a reason behind Mum's sudden attack of house proudness, but he was hoping it had come from a place of perhaps wanting to do it, rather than having to. Clip-boardy people had always come to the house. Especially when he was little. And, to be fair, the place probably had been a death-trap, despite his mum's attempts to keep him safe. He used to pretend to be a racing car speeding around the narrow corridors as if he were taking part in the world's fastest race. The clip-boarders would worry about rats and smells, but Marty never saw anything wrong with rats and smells. It was the stone-throwing kids from up the road that worried him more, and the angry man with his red face that kept shouting over the garden wall about 'disgrace' and 'bringing down the value of everyone's properties'. The rats, in comparison, had always seemed kind of friendly.

Marty took the letter and started to read. He scanned

it quickly. They knew this day might come. Over time, the warnings had become threats of legal action. And the threats of legal action meant that Marty always had to answer the door just in case and say his mum wasn't at home, which was ironic really because she was never out, but nothing concrete had ever really come of it. Until now . . .

'Oh my God, Mum, they're coming next week . . .'

Mum shrugged her shoulders. 'We've got plenty of time.'

'We're on our last warning, Mum. They'll throw us out and then what'll we do?'

His mum pretended not to hear. 'We're almost there; we've only got a few more bits to go . . .'

'*A few more bits?*'

'Don't use that tone with me, Marty.'

'I'm not – it's just that . . .'

Mum had turned stony-faced again. Her eyes had cooled. She looked away.

'Anyway, isn't it time you were off to school?'

She was right. He was late. He got up.

'Listen, Mum, I didn't mean to . . . It's just such a lot

31

of work . . . and we've only got a week . . .'

He could see that the fog had started to come back across her face already.

'I do try, you know . . .'

Marty's stomach tied in a knot. 'I know . . . I know . . . and, as you say, we've got a little time . . .'

'So thanks for the fish smell.'

Marty's face fell. 'What?'

It was Gracie, the annoying girl, again.

'Thanks to your allotment, my clothes, my coat. *Everything* stinks of fish . . .'

'What . . . ? Where . . . ?' He watched as she sat down.

'I live behind the allotments,' she spelled out to him slowly, as if he had precisely three and a half brain cells. 'I left my bedroom window open last night and now everything in my house stinks of fish . . .'

Marty began to mount a defence for himself.

'Don't even try and say it wasn't you, because I saw you there – and your uncle? Grandad?'

Marty's shoulders fell in defeat. 'Grandad . . .'

He wanted to shrink. Shrink away and disappear.

'And by the way –' she leaned over and sniffed the shoulder of Marty's jumper – 'just so you know, you don't smell so good either.'

Marty lifted his arm across his nose and took a good sniff of his jumper. This day just could not get any worse. He had eaten his lunch quickly, gobbling down the food, hardly tasting a thing so he could go and sit outside and think about how he and his mum were going to clear a whole house in a couple of days. And now, on top of everything, he stank of fish . . .

'It's my grandad. He makes fish gunk and he bought me this seed for my birthday and he really wants it to grow and . . .' Marty noticed Gracie was looking at him funny.

'Er, yeah, don't worry about it,' she said.

They sat for a moment in silence, just stinking of fish.

'You must be posh, then . . .' he said eventually.

'What?'

'Living in one of those houses? They're huge.'

She shrugged. 'They're all right.'

Marty knew he shouldn't have asked, but the words came out of his mouth before his brain cells kicked into gear.

'So, how does that thing work, then?' He nodded to Gracie's cochlear implant.

She rolled her eyes at him. 'Your social skills are spectacular.'

'I mean, the deafness. Does it fix it?'

'I don't need fixing, thanks . . .'

'Er, well, yeah, I know that. It's just that . . .' Marty tailed off; she had a knack of pushing him to some really awkward places in his head.

Gracie was quiet a moment.

'The processor behind my ear turns sound into electrical signals, and this here –' she pointed to the button thing – 'is a transmitter coil . . .'

She pushed her hair back.

'It's kept in place with a magnet so I can take it off if I want to.'

Marty's mind was whirring.

'That is pretty cool . . .' he said.

Gracie looked at him in a bemused way.

'It's not perfect,' she said eventually. 'I can switch it off too, which I do sometimes, especially when it's maths . . . or when there are really stupid people about . . .'

Marty laughed. He didn't do that much at school. It was more of a 'get there and get out' situation for him. He had tried to make a few friends before. Some of the other kids were actually OK. It was just they tended to play computer games together and Marty didn't have those, or they would go to each other's houses at the weekends and Marty could never have anyone back, so any effort he made with them just kind of petered out.

'The bell rang . . .' Marty said.

'I know.' She smiled.

Marty got up. 'I've got double maths . . .'

'I'm going that way too . . .'

Marty shifted his weight from one foot to the other.

'Well, we may as well walk together, then . . .' he suggested as he watched Gracie get up. 'Since we both stink . . .' he added.

Gracie walked past him and muttered . . . 'Such a charming way with words too.'

CHAPTER FIVE

'What do you think?'

Marty felt his stomach lurch. It was phenomenal. Less than a week had gone by, but the seed had sprouted. It had split in two and sent down long white sucker roots that were just about visible digging into the soil. From the top end, two leaves had shot upward. Triangular and sort of deep green. Marty reached out to touch them and, as he did, he felt a quivering deep down in his tummy.

'Those are the pilot leaves,' explained Grandad, watching him. 'They will power the roots with energy until the plant really gets going . . .'

'But it's grown so fast!' exclaimed Marty.

Grandad grinned.

'Indeed it has! Indeed it has!' He was jumping around and clapping his hands. 'But you ain't seen nothing yet, son!'

'What on earth is it?' asked Marty. 'Come on, you've GOT to tell me now . . .'

Grandad was enjoying this and tapped the side of his nose mysteriously.

'You'll see . . .'

'Oh, please?'

'Nope, sorry, kid. Go on, then,' Grandad said. 'I mean, go and make the tea for your old grandad.'

Marty reluctantly turned away from the plant and walked to the shed.

He had been thinking whether he should tell Grandad about Mum. About the letter from the council. About how she'd been clearing out. About how even the kitchen looked passable now. She'd taken all the bags of stuff out to the back garden and hidden them under the back-room carpet, which she'd ripped out because it had looked so stained and awful. There was a tiny little bit of pride in him that wanted her to prove her dad wrong, but he couldn't quite bring himself to tell him. Just in case.

Marty boiled the kettle, fished out a couple of teabags and looked at the map of the world that Grandad had pinned up on the inside wall of the garden shed. The geography teacher at school had had a bright idea one day and hung a map of the world on the back of the classroom door in school. He had asked everyone to mark on it with little stars the places they had been. The point of the exercise was to see how many places the pupils of 9D had been to collectively so that they could learn about them. Marty thought that it had probably been a good idea in Mr Philpott's head. Helen had been skiing in the Alps. Thomas had family in Canada, so he put a star there. Cassie had been almost everywhere, because her dad had a home in America and they holidayed all over the place. Marty had hesitated, before putting a star over the town of Brighton. His grandad had taken him there one day. Only for the day, and it had taken so long to get there on the bus that they only had a couple of hours to see the Royal Pavilion and have an ice cream before having to come back again.

Grandad's map was shabbier and curled at the edges from damp, but he had put his initials on the places

where he wanted to go. Paris. Italy. There were pictures of him pinned to the wall of the shed too. In his old railway uniform. He'd gone back and forth in straight lines between cities for years and years, so perhaps it did make some sense that now, in retirement, he wanted to go his own way.

Marty had never known his grandma. Grandad had been married to her about five years before Marty's mum was born and then things had kind of fallen apart. Grandad was always hatching schemes and plans that would end up not working or even actually costing them money, and they had rent to pay and she'd be working long hours and Marty could imagine her getting fed up with him. The one thing that Grandad did very well, though, was to kind of be there. Just at the side of Marty's vision. A kind of constant spot in the way that he looked at the world that gave perspective on everything else. He also told him stories, not ones from books, but ones from his head. Silly, wonderful stories.

'How's that tea coming along?'

Grandad was pulling off his gardening gloves. Marty handed him his enamel mug and wondered why anyone would decide to make a mug out of a material that got so finger-burningly hot. Grandad peered over Marty's shoulder at the map.

'One day, my son, we'll go to Paris . . . see that tower you've always wanted to see . . .'

'Do you think it's as wonderful as it looks in the pictures?' Marty asked.

He could feel his grandad's raspy breaths behind him.

'I reckon it's probably even more wonderfuller.'

Marty smiled. Ever since he'd been old enough to know that the model Dad had given him was of an actual place, an actual tower, he'd always wanted to visit it. He couldn't remember much about his dad. It was more just scraps of memories. The raspy scratchiness of his chin when he kissed him. Being thrown in the air and caught. Mum and Dad shouting at each other. He did, however, remember his dad pressing the model of the Eiffel Tower into his hands on his fourth birthday. Saying he loved him as tall as a tower. No explanation. Nothing. That was the last time he'd seen him. And he'd often wondered how you could love someone as tall as a tower and still disappear. And over the years his desire to see the tower itself had grown and grown and grown. Sometimes, when Marty was lying in bed, feeling the weight of all the stuff on him, he'd think about climbing it. Step after step. Going up, up, up into the world.

'Come on, son.' His grandad pulled at his shoulder.

'So how are we going to reach Paris when we can't even afford the bus fare into town?' asked Marty as he followed him out into the garden.

Grandad tapped the side of his nose with his finger.

'Don't you worry about things like that – they're all details. Details. Piffling little details.'

Grandad sat down with a creak.

'So how's school going?'

Marty shrugged.

'Still swearing at those kids under your breath?'

'Yup.'

'Good boy . . .'

'Got any friends?'

Marty hesitated.

'Maybe . . .'

Grandad knocked back his trilby with the side of his hand and raised his eyebrows. A slow smile started to cross his face.

'Well, that's good – that's really good . . . What's his name?'

'*Her* name is Gracie . . .' said Marty, looking at his feet.

'Gracie?' pondered Grandad.

'I was thinking that maybe she could come and look at the seed, maybe . . . I mean, it doesn't matter. I haven't asked her or anything . . .'

'That'd be lovely,' said Grandad, clearly enjoying himself. 'There's only one problem, though . . .'

Marty's forehead twisted into a question.

'What?'

'You'll have to tell her to bring her own mug . . .'

Gracie arrived home and shouted, just in case, like she always did.

'In here!' a distracted voice came back.

Gracie smiled. Threw her keys on the side table and dropped her bag on the floor. The hallway was high-ceilinged, grand, with cold geometric tiles on the floor. All the walls were painted white. Her dad was working on his laptop on the kitchen table. He didn't look up.

'I didn't think you'd be here,' Gracie said as she stood in the kitchen doorway.

Her dad continued tapping away.

'I'm not. Not really. I just slipped home to get some files. I'm just an illusion.'

Gracie smiled silently at her father, his eyes glued to the screen.

'How was school anyway?' he asked.

Gracie shrugged.

'It was OK . . .'

'How was Poppy and your other mates?'

Gracie studied him. It was always easier
to lie when no one looked into your eyes.

'Fine.'

Gracie's dad typed his last message and closed his
laptop. He pulled off his glasses.

'OK, that's done.'

He looked at his watch and blew out his cheeks.

'There's some food in the fridge.'

Gracie's heart fell. She knew what that meant. The
negotiations were about to start.

'You don't mind if I have dinner with Louise tonight, do you?'

Gracie got on with her dad all right. It was just that sometimes he talked to her like an adult. Which might sound like a strange thing to complain about when most kids just want to be taken a little bit more seriously, but it was almost as if her dad had already checked out of being, well, a dad.

'No, that's fine.'

'You're old enough to cater for yourself, aren't you?'

'Course I am.'

'I'll only be on the other side of the phone.'

Gracie smiled and watched as her dad slid his computer into its case, tipped himself off the stool and whipped his jacket off the nearby chair. He shunted his arms into the sleeves and straightened his collar.

'You know I'm doing this for us, right?'

Gracie nodded. 'I know.'

'Setting up a new business takes time . . . but it's an investment. For our future . . .'

Gracie smiled.

'You got homework?' he asked.

Gracie nodded.

'Better get to it, then . . .' he suggested.

He moved towards Gracie and kissed her head.

'Have you grown again?' he asked, and then he was gone.

Gracie watched the door shut behind him and went to sit on the squeaky leather sofa overlooking the allotments beyond the garden, the starkness of the room a direct contrast to the messy, jungly patchwork of people and plants outside. Her dad had had the lawn taken up and replaced with plastic grass, the borders of which were sharp. Defined. Unnatural.

She was old enough to 'cater' for herself. She knew that. It was just that sometimes she didn't want to. Yes, he'd occasionally take her for a nice meal, but sometimes she longed for them to eat pizza on the floor in front of the telly so that they could watch cartoons together. It was as if he were in a constant negotiation with Gracie about how little she should need him. She was loved. Gracie knew that, but since her parents divorced, her dad had kind of ploughed all his time into his new business and buying bigger and bigger houses, like this one, for them to rattle about in and, to be honest, she hardly saw him. Her mum rang or messaged her every day, but, since she had remarried and had kids with Jeffrey, Gracie kind of preferred the quietness of Dad's house rather than the chaos at Mum's. Dad and Mum didn't talk to each other, except through their lawyers, and both were clinically polite about each other when talking to Gracie. Sometimes, Gracie wished they would shout. Lie. Throw things. Cry. Do *something*. But they were just terribly, terribly *nice*.

Gracie looked out at the allotments. It was getting darker now, the shadows lengthening. She had spent the afternoon in IT lessons longing for the teacher's drone to end and, having waited for Marty and not seen him, had made her way home alone. She could feel the knots in her neck where she had strained to keep up in class. Even though the teachers gave her extra time at the end of every lesson to process what they'd done, it was still hard going. Her dad had been keen that she attend a 'normal' school. Whatever that meant. From what she could tell, she hadn't met anyone very 'normal' there. He was always so supportive, so determined that her deafness shouldn't 'hold her back' that he pushed her. Really hard. Her head was heavy with words and sentences and thinking, and she decided to clear it the only way she knew how. She kicked off her shoes and her jumper. Sat on the sofa and peeled off her socks. The marble floor was cold beneath her feet. She leaned her full weight on the sofa and pushed it back so she had room to move. Then, she asked the smart speaker for some music, turned the music up to ten, clicked off her processor and stood in the middle of the house. Feeling. Feeling. She exhaled, a slow smile spreading as she felt the music start to take over her body.

CHAPTER SIX

M arty had bought three packs of extra-strong rubbish bags. The cheap ones from the pound shop just wouldn't cut it. He had decided he would start in the back corridor, where he would fill two bags at a time and then cycle them all the way to the dump, the bags tied to the handlebars of his BMX. Then, when he was there, all the way at the other side of town, he would chuck them over the dump wall as no one under sixteen was allowed on site. Which was stupid, but they were the rules, and there was a weaselly little man in a high-vis jacket who would keep on trying to catch him.

He'd managed eight whole bags so far, but, to be honest, he hadn't made a dent in the stuff. His mother was concentrating on sorting out the kitchen, but every time she seemed to be making progress more stuff would just seem to appear. It seemed that everything was compressed together and the more you cleared, the more stuff you found.

The worst thing, however, about the whole exercise was that to get to the dump he had to pass the housing estate on the other side of town where all the 'new-trainer kids' lived. They'd clocked him passing back and forth on his bike and had come to hang about on the corner, waiting for him. There was Gerry, the thinnest and the tallest, who always had the new phone and the new games. And then a shorter dark-haired one called Owen; he was a right pain in the backside. Marty didn't know the others. Of course, they were going to laugh – Marty wasn't expecting them to do anything else – but they were also shouting out horrible, nasty things.

'Your mum still alive in that house?'

'Bet she's dead under all that rubbish . . .'

'Look! It's trash carrying trash!'

Marty kept on riding his bike, swearing like a trooper under his breath all the way. He tried going a different route, but it still brought him back to this one-way road to the dump. It was hard enough as it was – balancing two bags of rubbish and cycling forward at the same time. He'd try to fill each bag to the same level so that the weight was equal – that much he had learned in physics – but it was still a tricky operation without people shouting things that made your blood boil. If they could only make the place presentable, they could convince the council that they were doing something. Taking action. Maybe that would be enough to convince them to leave them alone for another little while.

He didn't actually see the stick coming. The aim was pretty spectacular; even Marty had to admit that. It jammed into the spokes of his wheels and sent Marty flying, the two bags of rubbish sailing through the air past his ears and bursting like trashy waterbombs all over the road. His chin skidded across the gravel, the spiky pain of blood held off a moment by shock. He didn't know where he was or what had happened. The new-trainer kids laughed, and filmed Marty sitting in the middle of the road, shock on his face and rubbish all around him.

Something inside Marty snapped. He got up and, almost without him even realizing what he was doing, he walked towards Gerry and hit him hard in the face. Gerry promptly cried, then got back on his bike and cycled home to tell his mum, followed by all the others. Marty stood there a moment, his chest heaving, anger coursing through his blood before becoming aware of a drone, a nagging voice, someone shouting angrily. It was getting nearer and nearer. It was the weaselly dump man shaking his fist and shouting at Marty to clear up the mess.

Marty had never been in the head's office before. He'd known it was coming even before he came to school the next morning. It was inevitable, really. And then he'd seen Gerry outside the head's office, a bruise on his face, sitting next to his protective mum, her arm round him. There was no point lying.

Miss James looked across her desk at him, her bored eyes speaking of someone who had been a head teacher far too long. All the kids were terrified of her, which, on the surface of it, was quite weird as she was just a little old lady, but there was a poison in the looks she gave you that could wither you at a hundred paces. Marty could tell that even the teachers were scared of her, especially the new ones. School legend had it that she even gave them lines as punishment if they disobeyed her. *Actual* lines! Marty had often wondered exactly how old she was. Gracie's first impression had been around ninety. Marty had thought that was a bit of an exaggeration, but now that he was close to her he wasn't so sure. She had a weary slowness about her that made her look like some kind of ancient owl. She looked at him as if he were a mouse in her talons that she was about to casually rip apart.

'I really am disappointed in you, Marty,' she began.

Marty was surprised that she even knew his name. He wasn't on the football team, was never up for any awards. To be honest, apart from Mr Garraway, Marty doubted if anyone at school knew he even existed. Her eyes took in his scabby chin. He'd dunked it in water when he'd got home. Told Mum he'd fallen off his bike, which was actually technically true. It still felt tight and stingy even though it had started to scab over.

'Very disappointed indeed.'

She sniffed her beak-like nose, and shuffled a few papers, before reaching for a cream cracker from a small plate on her desk. Marty watched as she shoved one into her mouth and started to chew sourly.

'I've seen many a boy like you go down a terrible path.'

As she talked, she scattered bits of dry cracker everywhere. Marty tried to push his chair back a little.

'This is how it starts. Trouble. Here and there. And before you know it you're on a slippery slope.'

She looked up at him through her hooded eyelids.

'Now tell me, boy –' she'd stopped chewing now – 'did Gerry do that to you?' She was pointing a long knobbly finger, her nail painted in a thick layer of scarlet nail varnish towards his chin now.

Marty contemplated this for a moment. Had the boy punched him? No. Had he been responsible for Marty falling. Well, sort of. Would Marty have fallen if he wasn't there? No. Was he the one that threw the stick? Marty couldn't be sure.

'Marty?' came her voice again.

Marty shook his head.

'No . . .'

She sat back for a moment. Drummed her long fingernails on the desk. Marty noticed she had three hairs growing out from under her chin. Each of them stiff and slightly curly. She looked at him again with narrowed eyes.

'Hmm, I am displeased. Disappointed. Annoyed. These things don't reflect well on the school.'

Marty sat, awaiting his fate as she reached for another cracker, wishing the ordeal was over. The phone began to ring on her desk. Her eyes barely registered it as she sat chewing, squishy cracker gunk collecting in the corners of her mouth.

'Since this is the first time you've been in trouble,' she said in her slow, laborious voice, 'and the incident happened outside of school, we'll leave it with a good week of lunchtime detention. BUT –' she leaned forward at this – 'if anything else happens, and I mean *anything*, then we'll have to get your mother in.'

Marty laughed involuntarily. Miss James's eyebrows darted upward like two surprised caterpillars.

'What was that?'

'Nothing . . .'

'It wasn't what I'd call *an attitude*, was it?'

'No, miss.'

Marty doubted that anyone could actually get his

mother out of the house, but, looking at Miss James's beady eyes, he was sure she'd give it a damn good try.

'Right, then, you're dismissed.'

She waved her hand and Marty got up, still aching all over. He listened as she snatched up the phone behind him and answered with an irritated, 'Yeeeeeeeessss?'

Marty pushed the door open and stepped into the schoolyard. It was morning break and the kids were lining up at the tuck shop. He heard the laughter as he walked past. They were all looking at their phones and Marty knew what they were watching. Gerry, who had been tucked under his mum's arm just minutes before, had transformed back into the gangly orangutan that he usually was. He seemed to have grown almost a metre and was pointing at Marty and laughing.

'Have a good trip, did you?'

'You look better now that your face is smashed up a bit,' Gerry's friend wisecracked.

Marty tried not to listen. He carried on walking.

He was actually exhausted. Absolutely exhausted. He had worked through the night trying to make a difference

in the house. Brushing. Scrubbing. Emptying the bath. His mother, though, had started the hand-wringing again, but he knew she was trying not to say anything as he moved things out to the garden.

He knew the man from the council would be there by now. He knew it and it had been on his mind every second of the day. He had wondered whether he should skive off school to meet him, but had decided that it would probably make him question them more. The best thing he could do was stay away and hope. Hope that Mum could hold it together long enough for the council to be convinced that she intended to do something about the mess this time . . .

Marty had just about reached the wall behind the French department, where he'd planned on hiding for the rest of break, when he heard a voice behind him.

'I saw the video . . . It's rubbish,' she joked.

It was Gracie. Her crooked smile would usually make a smile spread on his face too.

'I'm not in the mood, OK?'

'Oh, come on, Marty. It's pretty funny. What on earth were you doing?'

'Oh, it's hilarious . . .' he spat. 'My life is hilarious, isn't it? And now everyone knows that I'm the loser that I am . . .'

He started walking back towards the school.

'Marty?' She was pulling at his shoulder now. 'Stop.'

'No!' He shrugged off her hand. 'Just not now, OK, Gracie?'

She stopped then and he was glad that she had, because

he was suddenly hot with anger and his voice was tight and trembly in his throat. He pushed the school doors open and made a promise to himself to ignore everyone until the bell rang at the end of the day.

Marty's stomach was tight and hard as he pushed open the back door. He'd been playing different scenarios in his head all the way home. In one, he'd come home and Mum would be crying in her chair, letters on the floor all around her, stamped with words like BAILIFF and NOT ENOUGH PROGRESS and things like that. In another, she'd be bouncing up and down, happy as Larry, telling him that they were going to be all right. He braced himself and pushed his way in.

He hadn't actually prepared for this one. Mum was sitting in her chair, yes, but she wasn't laughing or crying. She just looked really serious. Marty dropped his bag, walked towards her. She lifted her head to look at him.

'So?' he asked. She'd made an effort with her clothes. She'd tied her hair back.

'They're letting us stay here.'

Marty let out a deep breath of relief. He laughed before

studying her. Her stillness was making him nervous.

'But that's good . . . That's good, isn't it?'

'Yes . . .' Her eyes were darting all over the place. 'Marty, sit down . . .'

These were never good words. Not when your friend said them or your mum or a teacher. You kind of knew something serious was coming. Marty sat on the floor by her chair.

'I've been thinking, Marty . . . about what I've put you through . . .'

Marty looked at the floor.

'About how you've had to live here, like this, with me . . .'

Marty hated talking about this stuff. He swallowed hard, his head feeling light and his thoughts sliding everywhere.

'It's OK, Mum . . .'

'No, it's not . . .' She looked at him, her eyes welling with tears. 'I've been sitting here feeling ashamed of myself . . .'

'Please, don't . . .'

'And I want to make you a promise . . .'

Marty hated these words.

'Once and for all, this has been the push that I've needed . . .'

'Don't, Mum . . .'

'I promise you . . . Marty, look at me . . . I promise you that I will sort this out once and for all . . . We'll have a nice . . . normal house. You'll have a nice, normal mum . . .'

All the words Marty wanted to say just got jammed in his throat, so many wanting to come out at the same time that they kind of all got stuck, so he said nothing at all. He nodded, tears prickling his eyes.

'Now,' she said, getting up, 'let me get us some dinner.'

CHAPTER SEVEN

'I'm sorry, OK?'

Gracie came to sit next to him on the wall. Marty could see from her face that she meant it. He'd been let out of detention early and had come to the back of the languages block to hide until lunchtime was over. Marty ignored her as she sat down, hugging her school bag in her lap. They sat in silence for a moment. She was looking straight ahead.

'I know I can be a bit . . .' She hesitated. 'You know. Harsh.'

Marty gave a soft smile.

'R-e-a-l-l-y?' he said, and raised an eyebrow.

Gracie smiled.

'It's just . . . I've kind of had people say stuff about me

all my life. Behind my back –' she gave a tight laugh – 'to my face, even. I suppose you learn to say something before anyone else does.'

Marty looked at her. She seemed almost sad.

'Ignore them.' She was studying her hands now. 'They're not worth it. That's what I've learned over the years, anyway.'

Marty sat in silence for a moment, listening as Gracie kicked her heels against the wall.

'I'm sorry too. I've just got some stuff on my mind. That's all.'

Gracie nodded. Didn't ask any more.

'We friends?' she said at last.

Marty studied her.

'Yes.'

'Good . . .'

Marty felt his shoulders soften. Gracie grabbed his sleeve.

'Because I want to show you something.'

Marty had never been to the other side of the school car park before. Had never even noticed the wall. It ran in a perfect curve, an even half-circle, all the way round the trees in front of it. It was graffitied, of course, but was in all other ways completely unremarkable until Gracie showed him something.

'Stand there,' she said, turning him sideways and placing him at one end of the wall.

'Why?'

She smiled. 'You'll see.'

She walked the demi-curve of the wall and stood at the other side. And there she did something remarkable! She whispered. Marty listened as her quiet voice bounced and bounced along the wall, getting louder and louder and louder! *WHOOSH!*

'HELLLLLLLLLLLLLLOOOOOOOOOOO!'

Marty jumped out of his skin. It was as if she were shouting into his ear, yet she was standing SO far away! He smiled, his eyes coming alive and the hair on the back of his neck bristling.

'IT'S AMAZING, ISN'T IT? A WHISPERING WALL!'

Marty laughed, and whispered back at her, 'HOW DID YOU FIND IT?'

'I'M A GENIUS!'

Marty grinned.

They stood in silence for a moment until Gracie spoke again.

'CLOSE YOUR EYES! AND LISTEN.'

Marty did as he was told.

'THIS IS HOW I FEEL SOUND,' she said.

Marty felt the words on his face, vibrating in his head.

'IN MY BODY.'

Marty beamed, his eyes still closed.

'MUSIC . . . BLOWS . . . MY . . . MIND.'

Then came her voice again. More hesitant this time. Less together. Less sure. Less directed.

'I WANT TO BE A DANCER.'

A confession. Then silence.

'I'VE NEVER, EVER TOLD ANYONE THAT BEFORE. IT'S STUPID, EH? I MEAN, I'M DEAF . . .'

Marty thought about it. Thought about sound. He thought about the vibrations in his house, about how still it was and how difficult it was to feel free. And then he thought about dancing, and it seemed to make sense.

'I THINK YOU'LL MAKE A TERRIFIC DANCER. THE BEST.'

CHAPTER EIGHT

'Cabbage?' suggested Gracie.

Marty rolled his eyes. 'Seriously? Whoever saw a cabbage that tall before?'

'Erm, ooh, I know. A Brussels sprout plant . . .' Gracie tried again.

Grandad shook his head.

Gracie crossed her arms. 'I give up.'

'Me too,' agreed Marty. 'Why don't you just tell us?'

'Patience!' he said, raising his eyebrows mischievously. 'It's a good lesson, short stuffs!'

The plant was now up to Grandad's chest. It really was wondrous. Its two leaves had tripled overnight and now six strong leaves were unfurling palms upward towards the sun. Even though it was still quite cold, you could feel summer in the air today. It was a tie-your-jumper-in-a-knot-round-your-waist kind of day.

'When did you plant it?' asked Gracie.

'Only a couple of weeks ago.'

Gracie pulled a breath in through her teeth. 'That thing's a monster!'

'Let's hope so!' said Grandad.

They helped Grandad for a while. A lot of the other vegetables were going into the ground now as the soil began to warm up. There were cumin-shaped carrot seeds to sow in rows and little gnarly beetroot seeds like tiny little rocks to place in the soil one by one. There were also peas to plant, which looked exactly like, well, dried peas. Grandad would plant those in triangle formations so that he could tie them to sticks when they germinated. The blackcurrant bush had started to green out, and so had the gooseberry plant. Just a few weeks more, and summer would most definitely be on the way.

They'd worked for an hour or two at least before Grandad went to fill the kettle. Gracie had brought a mug from her house. A white china one with *Gracie* written in gold double writing on it. A personalized gift from her father.

'So, was it you that hit him?' Grandad asked Gracie, nodding towards Marty, as the three of them settled down with their tea.

Gracie cottoned on quickly. 'No, it wasn't me. Apparently loads of people don't like him, not just me.'

Marty could tell that Grandad liked Gracie; he was sitting back, relaxed, open-armed and smiley.

'I fell out with the floor,' Marty lied.

Grandad studied his face, but changed the subject.

'So, what you kids up to on Saturday?'

Marty shrugged. So did Gracie. They watched as Grandad pulled out a twenty-pound note from the top pocket of his jacket.

'Muggins 'ere found a scratch card in the middle of town. And bing, bang, bosh. Twenty quid. Now, we've got four months to get that plant as big as we can – all my plans rely on it – and on Saturday we're going on a field trip. Bus stop on Albany Road. Eight o'clock in the morning. Sharpish.'

Gracie looked at Marty and shrugged. 'OK.'

*

'So? What do you think it is, then?' pondered Gracie.

Marty walked up the path to Gracie's house, trying not to look shocked at how big it was.

'I don't know.'

'I have never seen a plant grow that fast. I mean, is that even normal?'

Marty had thought and thought about the seed and every time he thought about it, his fingertips would tingle.

'I just don't get it, that's all . . .' Gracie looked serious as she fumbled in her pocket for her key. Marty watched her open the door, the vast hallway swinging into view.

He'd been thinking about it and she was right. It didn't actually feel possible.

'It must be some hybrid or something,' he said. 'A quick-growing cross of two plants, perhaps? I read about it in Biology once. You can cross plants and they take on each other's characteristics.'

Gracie looked unconvinced as she stood in the doorway.

'Can I tell you something?' Her face was suddenly serious.

Marty looked at her. 'Of course . . .'

'Promise you won't laugh?'

'I promise.'

'I felt really weird when I was near it. I dunno. It's like I got really nervous or something.'

Marty's skin prickled. He had, of course, felt exactly the same. He frowned. It made no sense.

'Did you feel it?' She was looking at him now, but Marty looked away.

'It must be because we don't know what it is.' He was pulling up excuses now from deep down. 'Sometimes, things take on a magic or something because they seem mysterious, but they're actually normal. It's all normal. It's just in our heads.'

Gracie frowned. 'Do you really believe that?'

Marty shrugged.

Gracie looked at him hesitantly.

'Want to come in?' she offered. 'Dad's out. We could watch some TV.'

Marty shook his head from force of habit more than anything.

'I'm all right,' he answered, and looked back towards

the allotment. 'I'd better get back.'

Gracie shrugged. 'OK.'

Marty smiled. 'I'll see you tomorrow.'

'Sure,' Gracie replied, and closed the heavy door.

Marty turned and stood for a moment. In the distance, he could see Grandad still pottering about, his hat on his head and the enormous plant unfurling itself in the late light.

CHAPTER NINE

'Marty, Marty, Marty! In my room, please!'

Marty stopped dead in the corridor so that his trainers squeaked on the floor. It was Mr Garraway, the school counsellor. He was a huge, bear-like Scottish man with red hair and a penchant for shiny, tight tracksuits. He taught PE and health and well-being and talked very, very quickly about very, very embarrassing things. He was hanging by one arm from the door frame of his classroom. Marty looked back along the corridor where Gracie stood waiting for him. Mr Garraway read his mind. This was why he was so dangerous. He had an uncanny knack of knowing what you were thinking.

'Come on, come on, come on. Won't be long, sonny.'

Marty shrugged in Gracie's direction and she waved,

signifying that she'd see him later. He made his way into Mr Garraway's class, which was lavishly decorated with posters of Scotland and the different types of tartan. Marty gingerly sat on the edge of one of the desks as Mr Garraway closed the door.

He watched as Mr Garraway rubbed his bristly beard.

'I heard you had a run-in, shall we say?' He was looking at Marty's healing chin now. 'You OK?'

Marty nodded.

'None of my business, of course, but you give me a shout if you need to talk about anything . . .'

'OK,' Marty answered, fiddling with the strap of his rucksack.

'I know I'm not supposed to come down on anyone's side in any disputes, but, between you and me, that Gerry is a pain in the proverbial.'

Marty smiled and wondered whether that was it, until Mr Garraway piped up again.

'I've heard on the grapevine too – been given, shall we say, the heads-up, the nod – that you've not been handing in your homework, lad.'

Marty could never tell if Mr Garraway had finished speaking or not because he never seemed to come to a conclusion in a sentence.

'I'm not worried about you, obviously, but you *are* on my radar . . .'

Marty waited.

'That is to say, I'm looking out for you . . .'

He was definitely finished now. If Marty was brutally honest, homework and projects had been the furthest things from his mind. He hadn't even thought about them. Since he'd been clearing out the house, homework was so far down his list of 'things that are important', it had kind of fallen clean off the page. He considered quickly whether brutal honesty was the way forward or the more traditional approach of lying through his teeth. Mr Garraway was still staring at him.

'I just wanted to know whether I could help you out a little bit. Help you along. Find a solution for you. Maybe. I mean, give you a little advice . . .'

Marty tried going down the 'vagueness personified' route, to see if it would work. He shrugged. 'I'm sorry, I've just been really busy.'

Mr Garraway studied him for a moment. 'How's your ma these days?'

Marty tensed a little. Mr Garraway was good. He was really, really good.

'She's well,' he said eventually. 'Really well, actually.'

Mr Garraway studied him again. Could tell he wasn't lying. Was reassured.

'Good. Good,' he said. 'Grand. Aye, that's grand.'

Marty always felt a sense of guilt around Mr Garraway.

He knew that the teacher knew about his home life. Not that they'd ever talked properly about it, but information about kids like Marty was always passed on. Marty knew that. He also knew that Mr Garraway was a nice man. Or seemed so. Marty was always wary, though. In his experience, letting people in ended up in them wanting to interfere. Yes, the way they were living wasn't ideal, but it was also all he had ever known, and Mum was really, really, really doing her best. He just didn't want anyone messing that up just now.

'Listen, Marty, I'm the middleman. You know that, don't you, sonny? I'm the messenger. I'm the buffer, if you like, between you and the powers that be, if you know what I mean and catch my drift . . .'

He was sounding cryptic now and Marty had a fleeting image of him as a secret agent. A ginger James Bond.

'Just turn some work in, will you? It'll get 'em off your back . . .'

Marty nodded. 'Thanks, sir.'

He turned to go, but Mr Garraway had not finished with him yet.

'Have you given any thought to your choices, by the way? What you want to do?'

Marty looked at him, not following his train of thought.

'You'll have to choose which subjects you want to carry on with soon . . .'

Marty hadn't actually thought about this.

'Doctor? Scientist? What's it to be?'

'I'm sorry?' Marty didn't quite understand what he was hearing. 'You think I could be those things?'

Mr Garraway frowned.

'Marty, you've got a good brain on you. A good brain can take you anywhere. Anywhere in the world. It's your responsibility to take that brain, that mind of yours, and see where it will go. Yes, you may not come from the poshest of places, but that doesn't change where you can end up. You have as much a chance as anyone else in the world.'

Marty didn't know why, but he could feel his heart beating in his chest. Grandad had told him that he could do anything he wanted, of course, but Marty thought that maybe he was just being nice.

'Don't box yourself in, lad. What do you like? What's your passion?'

Marty thought a moment. 'I don't know.'

Mr Garraway laughed. 'You don't know?' He tilted his head to look at him. 'What do you want to achieve?'

Marty stuttered, 'I don't know.'

It wasn't as if he didn't have dreams. Real dreams. Dreams of seeing the world. Seeing how people lived. The places they lived. The things they built. And he wanted to start with the Eiffel Tower. But how could he explain that? It was just there were so many things in his life. So many things that filled his house and his brain that he had never had time to actually think about what *he* wanted. Mr Garraway was still looking at him.

'It's OK. Don't worry about it, but just give it some thought. Some consideration, if you like. Ponder upon it, if you will.'

Marty nodded.

'Right, then,' he said as he started walking past Marty, 'I need a coffee.'

And just like that their chat was over. Mr Garraway

slapped him on the back with his enormous hand, almost winding him.

'Thanks, sir.'

'You're welcome, sonny.'

Mr Garraway strode out and along the corridor, leaving Marty still in the doorway, his head spinning.

Gracie lay on her bed later that night thinking about how to tell her dad she was off on an adventure with Marty and his grandad on Saturday. The only problem was that Dad positively and absolutely hated Marty's grandad. Not that they even knew each other properly. They'd only spoken to argue, really. Her dad referred to him as Bonkers Allotment Man. Gracie couldn't really blame him, as Marty's grandad was always lighting fires and burning things so that columns of smoke would waft into their pristine kitchen or he'd be at the allotment at some ungodly hour on a Sunday noisily hacking away at some wood with his axe. And, of course, there was the fish-stink fest. The chances of him agreeing to her going on a day trip with him were exactly less than a big fat zero. The only option left to her was to lie, or perhaps to let her father assume some things and not correct him.

When she'd first started at the school a few months ago, Dad had done his usual thing of contacting his vast network of business contacts and selecting a few friends for her. He'd invited them round to the house and ordered an obscene amount of pizza for everyone. There was Esther and Dahlia, and Poppy. And they were nice and liked to talk about their pet dogs and their horses. But there was just one slight problem. They were mind-numbingly boring. So boring that Gracie would find herself actually yawning and thinking about naps. So boring, in fact, that Gracie would rather spend the day in school all alone than hear any more about how one of them had trained 'Twinkles' to shake paws with her. Gracie always threw their names into the conversation at home, of course, just to throw her dad off the scent, and since everyone was so busy the parents very rarely organized hang-outs, which worked out very well for Gracie.

Gracie had practised what she was going to say about Saturday in her head, and decided to creep up to the home office and wait for a space between her dad's business calls.

She put her head round the door to have her dad hold

his hand up at her. He looked stressed. He was standing at the window, frowning. Gracie was sure her dad was actually getting shorter. She knew that she herself was growing, but it was more than that. It was as if all the hours hunched over his laptop had squished his back, making him look about thirty centimetres shorter. Gracie waited, hanging on to the doorknob, listening as the conversation waxed and waned. Eventually, her dad gestured towards the desk. Gave her a pen. Gracie couldn't believe her luck. She took some paper, and scribbled her message on it.

Can I go out with my friends tomorrow? I'll have my phone with me.

Her dad read the note over her shoulder and nodded. He smiled. Gracie smiled back and started to slink out of the room. Just as she was about to close the door, her dad put his hand over the phone.

'*Do you need any money?*' he mouthed.

Gracie shrugged.

'*Take some. My wallet's downstairs.*'

She closed the door behind her and let her shoulders drop. She hadn't even had to lie. She was going out with her friends tomorrow and, actually, she couldn't wait.

CHAPTER TEN

It was a bright, shiny Saturday. Marty had got up early, cycled to the bus stop and chained his bike to the railings. Grandad was there already. His best jacket on, patches of corduroy on its elbows. His trilby had been brushed and he looked dapper in his own ramshackle kind of way. Gracie was walking down the road. Well, not walking exactly, but kind of skipping-dancing. She wasn't even doing the classic don't-step-on-the-cracks thing. She was kind of, well, walk-dancing...

Grandad started to dance as she got nearer, grabbed her hand and leaned her back into a dramatic final pose before they burst out laughing. By Grandad's feet were six empty plastic buckets, which he picked up as the bus pulled up at the stop.

'All aboard!' Grandad shouted, smiling. 'Two under-six-year-olds and a pensioner please, driver!'

'Under six?' the driver asked, raising an eyebrow.

'Shh, yes, don't stare at them. Their mother is a six-foot-eight model and their dad is a basketball player and they get very conscious of their height.'

The driver laughed so hard he actually gave them a discount and Grandad thanked him profusely, called him a gentleman and doffed his trilby at him.

Marty was thrilled to be having a day out, and Mum had even given him some money to spend. He didn't want to tell Grandad about Mum and her promise. Not yet. He wanted to keep it close to his heart for a while and get used to the idea before telling him. It just all felt a bit new and fragile and Marty didn't want to add the weight of Grandad's expectation to it too soon, just in case. Marty sat behind Grandad and Gracie, listening to them chat, the warm May sunshine on his face.

She was telling him about not being able to hear. About how she was diagnosed with moderate hearing loss when she was around three and had to wear a tiny hearing aid, and how, over time, her hearing had begun to deteriorate. Her mum and dad had noticed that she didn't look at them any more when they talked. Or didn't jump when there was a loud noise behind her, and how eventually she got the cochlear implant to help her. After that, she'd had to re-learn sounds, from the beginning, because the implant made everything sound so different. Marty heard her telling him that sometimes it was difficult to live between the deaf and hearing worlds. It was the little things, she said. How it was easier for her to speak one to one as kids tended to talk over each other in groups, or how sometimes she'd miss the punchline of a joke and find herself having to ask someone to repeat it, which kind of killed the moment.

By the time they got to the seaside, Marty was itching to get some fresh air. They got off the bus by the prom and looked at Grandad.

'Now what?' asked Marty.

'Come with me . . .'

They marched all the way to the beach, and followed Grandad down on to the sand. Then they watched as he stood, stock still, on the tideline.

'Oh dear . . .' Grandad said.

Marty rolled his eyes at Gracie . . . *Here we go*, he thought.

'I forgot to check the tide times.'

Then Grandad looked at the waves.

'But it's all right; it's going out . . . I reckon we've got a couple of hours to kill.'

'A couple of hours to kill?' asked Gracie.

Marty thought she'd be annoyed, but her face lit up.

'Ooooh! I've got money for ice creams,' she said breathlessly. 'Can we go on a donkey?'

And so they spent a yellow, warm few hours doing things that Marty hadn't done . . . well . . . ever. Gracie laughed and laughed as she saw him on the donkey. They ate chips from paper cones while dangling their legs off the promenade and chucked any that were left over at the seagulls and then pretended to be terrified when they flew too near. Grandad even took off his jacket and opened the top buttons so his hairy chest was on display.

'Don't get too excited now, ladies!' he shouted to anyone who could hear. 'Control yourselves . . .'

Marty's cheeks blushed red as Gracie laughed, and then Marty and his grandad watched as Gracie danced on the beach, her feet kicking up the sand around her, her body moving as if it were full of water, tipping and turning in time to the waves. Marty had never seen a dancer before, not really. He'd seen people dance, of course – Grandad doing his shimmies and that kind of stuff – but not a real live person with dancing in them. With dancing in the way they moved their arms or tilted their head. Someone who could hear something in the world that he couldn't.

Marty watched her, the beach and time and the

world disappearing. There seemed to be nothing but the brushstrokes of her arms finding colours in the air around her and the rhythm of her feet. Marty and Grandad were transfixed as she made shapes and lines and then, when she eventually surfaced back into their world, she stopped, her hands still above her head, and looked up at them as if she were seeing them for the first time.

'Well, I'll be darned,' said Grandad reverently.

'Blimey,' replied Marty, still looking at her.

Then she kind of transformed back into the Gracie they knew – her body relaxed, she switched her sound processor back on – and she walked towards them and flopped down on to the sand, her breathing still ragged. Grandad considered her for a moment in awe.

'Gracie, that thing you did just there,' said Grandad, 'that was magical.'

Gracie looked away shyly.

'No, look at me,' he said.

Gracie's eyes found Grandad's.

'It was . . . *magical* . . .' he repeated.

They smiled warmly at each other and Marty was sure he saw Gracie grow a little.

'Now,' said Grandad, hauling himself creakily to his feet, 'if you two will excuse me, I need a cup of tea.'

Marty and Gracie watched as he straightened himself up and bowed theatrically before wandering off.

They sat in silence for a moment.

'It is lovely here, isn't it?' Gracie said dreamily.

Marty felt his legs warm on the sand.

'It is,' he answered, listening to the sea.

Gracie reached into her pocket and pulled out a small piece of paper that was a bit frayed around the edges. She opened it up and offered it to Marty. Marty smiled a question on his confused face.

'It's a competition. A dance competition. To win a place at the School of Dance in London.'

Marty read the flyer.

Gracie smiled. 'It's an open call for people to try.'

'That's amazing!' replied Marty. 'You've got to do it.'

Gracie's breath was slowing now, her cheeks still flushed pink. She was raking the sand between her legs with her fingers.

'What?' Marty asked. 'You're not going to try? Are you serious?'

Gracie was uncharacteristically quiet.

'It's just that . . . the other kids. They'll have had training. *Proper* training.'

Marty had never seen her looking so unsure.

'Mum and Dad, I asked them if I could have classes, but they were worried. They thought I'd make a fool of myself. Get picked on –' she shrugged – 'I don't know. So I've never been trained. Not properly. I've just done it myself.'

'But you're a brilliant dancer!'

'It doesn't count.'

'Oh, come on! Has your dad even *seen* you dancing?'

Gracie looked away again.

Marty was speechless. He turned towards her, touched her arm lightly. Something had happened since his chat with Mr Garraway. Nothing big. Nothing earth-shattering, but something had woken up inside Marty that he hadn't known was asleep.

'Listen, Gracie. You're the best dancer I've ever seen. Training or no training.' He sucked some air between his teeth. 'I don't even think they could teach someone to dance like you can. You have to try . . .' He looked at the flyer again. 'When's the audition?'

'End of summer.'

'You've got plenty of time!'

'What would Dad say?'

Marty smiled. Shrugged.

'I don't know,' he answered. 'Does he have to know?'

Gracie smiled. 'Maybe not.'

They grinned at each other until Marty heard someone shouting. He looked up. The tide had gone out far enough for Grandad to put his plan into action. He was standing down by the tideline waving at them frantically.

'Come on, troops!' he boomed across the beach.

'Could he be any more embarrassing?' Marty asked flatly.

'Probably not,' Gracie said as she stood up. 'But he's brilliant! Come on,' she said, putting her arm out to pull him up. 'Let's see what he's got in store for us.'

By the time they got down to the rock pools, Grandad had dropped his jacket on a nearby boulder, rolled up his sleeves and was filling the buckets with green and brown slimy seaweed. Marty looked at him in bewilderment.

'Come on!' he encouraged. 'Get stuck in!'

Gracie rolled up the sleeves of her dress and Marty pushed up the sleeves of his woolly jumper and they started gathering.

'Get all of it. All the different colours,' Grandad shouted.

Marty had never noticed before – I mean, it wasn't every day you spent hours with your head in seaweed – but there were all different types. There was a rubbery one that grew in long belts, and another one that was fine like hair, and one that grew in the shape of a tree but which had little bubbles in it that Marty supposed helped it float. He looked over at Gracie, who was hauling a particularly stubborn specimen from a rock.

Then, when the buckets were almost full, Grandad grabbed the bare-foot Gracie and dropped her feet-first into one bucket after another so she could pack down the seaweed. Marty laughed as she stamped, the seaweed squelching in undignified farts beneath her feet.

It took them another half hour to fill the buckets to the brim, then they stood back, admiring their hard work, each one breathless, the sun starting to sink slowly in the sky.

Gracie wiped her brow and looked over at Grandad.

'So? What now?'

'Shoes on –' Grandad grinned – 'and back on the bus! Two buckets each . . . Let's hope we won't have to pay the full fare for them . . .'

Nobody sat next to them. And, to be honest, Marty wasn't surprised by that. Not that the seaweed smelt bad or anything; it was just that you probably wouldn't choose to sit next to three people taking six buckets of seaweed on a bus trip.

'We're going to make our plant a cup of tea,' said Grandad.

'Tea?' Gracie raised an eyebrow.

'Soak this seaweed in water, leave it out in the sun and brew Marty's plant a nice refreshing cup of seaweed tea. I promise you. The thing'll grow bigger than a triffid.'

Gracie clearly still didn't know what he was talking about, but smiled anyway.

Marty was sitting in the window seat, watching the

seaside disappear and the green spaces become smaller and smaller as they got closer to the middle of the city. When they arrived, the three of them helped each other carry the seaweed back to the allotments (made easier by Marty's BMX). Afterwards, Gracie ran home and, once she had waved through her bedroom window to signal that she had arrived safely, Grandad walked Marty home.

Marty stopped at the gate.

'Want to come in?' he asked hopefully.

It was obvious that some clearing had been going on.

'No, you're all right,' Grandad said.

Marty nodded, trying not to add, '*Please?*'

'OK, goodnight, Marty boy.'

'Goodnight, Grandad.'

Marty watched Grandad disappear into the orangey light of the streetlamps before shouting after him, 'It was fun!'

Grandad turned and raised the trilby off his head a moment before saying, 'Of course it was!'

CHAPTER ELEVEN

Marty's mum had started washing clothes. That may not sound like such a big deal, but she had started washing clothes and hanging them on the washing line outside. The weather was getting warmer and the rubbish in the garden had started to really stink, but Marty couldn't have been happier. Marty watched her come in as he spread butter on some toast for them both. Mum sat down and took a sip of the tea that Marty had made her.

'So? Come on, tell me all about it!'

Marty looked at her in confusion.

'Yesterday, did you have fun?'

Marty smiled broadly. 'Yes.'

Marty wasn't sure, but he thought he saw a little disappointment in her face.

'I-I mean,' he stammered. 'It was OK.'

His mum smiled at him. Put down her cup. She studied him for a while.

'It's OK, you know. It's good for you to have fun . . .' She paused a moment. 'I want you to have fun.'

Marty smiled back softly. He wanted to say that he wished she'd been able to come too, but he didn't want to make her feel bad.

'You never know,' she said. 'One day, maybe next summer, I could come with you too.'

Marty nodded.

'How was Grandad?'

Whenever his mum said the word 'Grandad' it sounded a bit strange. A little prickly. It was like she'd just passed you a hedgehog and you had to be careful how you handled it.

'He bought me this seed. It was for my birthday.'

Mum was smiling.

'I don't even know what it is, but it's growing. This plant. It's enormous. I mean really enormous. He says we're going to use it for an adventure . . .'

Mum's smile fell a little. 'Typical Grandad.'

Marty felt her tone was a little dismissive.

'But really, Mum, I've never seen anything like it. It's growing and we went to the beach and collected seaweed to make it some tea.'

'*Tea?*'

'I know!' Marty laughed. 'He says he wants it to grow as big as a house.'

Mum listened as she chewed on her toast.

'Just remember that Grandad's plans tend not to end too well . . .'

Marty felt his chest sink.

'Not that . . .' she began. 'I didn't mean to throw cold water on anything, it's just that I've lived with his plans all my life . . .'

'I know,' answered Marty.

He watched his mum as she took another sip of her tea. Perhaps she was right. Perhaps it was something to do with the sun, or Gracie's dancing or something, but for a moment there he'd thought that Grandad might actually be on to something.

'Anyway, Gracie thinks . . .'

Mum lifted an eyebrow. 'Gracie?'

Marty had said her name before even thinking. He hadn't mentioned her before. Not really. He felt silly all of a sudden.

'She's my friend . . .' His voice was smaller now.

'I've never heard you mention her before?'

Marty shrugged. 'She lives by the allotments in one of those big houses. She's nice.'

A broad smile was spreading on his mum's face.

'Well, you should bring her around.'

'What, *here*?'

'Yes, here – where do you think?'

Marty looked around and, actually, there was less mess in the house now than there had ever been. His mum, for once, looked genuinely happy.

'It'd be nice for you. You know. To do what normal kids do. I can make you squash and biscuits.'

Marty hadn't told Gracie about his mum. About the house. He'd never really let anyone get as close to him as Gracie before, and although he'd thought about telling her many times he just didn't want to weigh her down with all of it. Marty had thought that she must already know *something*, what with all the rumours in school, but as they had never talked about it he could happily pretend the whole thing wasn't there.

'Marty? Are you going to let me meet her or what?' Mum asked.

Marty shrugged. 'Maybe.'

'*Pffft*, there's no *maybe* about it. Bring her over. It'll be fun.'

Marty had tried to ask Gracie about coming to the house for a few weeks, but every time he opened his mouth he'd somehow find himself changing the subject. It was nothing, really. Just asking her back for some squash. It wasn't anything major, but somehow, until now, he'd managed to keep school and home separate. He did trust Gracie – of course he did – it was just . . . It just felt *big*.

Marty hurried along the path, towards the school, where he knew Gracie would be waiting for him. He was late because he'd swung by the allotment and Grandad had shown him a bud on the plant that was absolutely enormous. It was fuzzy and torpedo-shaped, and almost as long as Marty's arm! Marty had gaped at it open-mouthed, trying to guess what colour the flower would be, thinking that it might give him at least a little clue as to what kind of plant it was . . . But no. Nothing. He'd pulled himself away from it eventually and had been racking his brains all the way to school, trying to guess what it was.

Marty turned the corner to see Gracie already by the wall.

'I'm so sorry I'm late,' gasped Marty.

Gracie rolled her eyes and smiled simultaneously.

'It's OK. You're here now.'

It was a Sunday afternoon, and the school felt totally different when it was empty. No shouting. No bag throwing. No Gerry and his mates. Just a deserted yard with a few empty crisp packets rustling across it. Marty watched as Gracie took off her jacket and threw it on the grass before placing her phone against the middle of the whispering wall. She pressed the screen and selected a song and went to stand, letting the music bounce along the wall in both directions so that it amplified the sound behind her.

Ever since dancing on the beach a few weeks ago, ideas for her audition had started to grow in Gracie's head. She hadn't sat down and thought about it or planned every move on paper – it didn't work like that for Gracie – but sometimes movements would come to her like thoughts or feelings, usually when she was doing something else. And those thoughts wouldn't make sense either. Not immediately. They were like syllables and sounds, or part words, but slowly, if she gave them enough space in her mind to grow, her body would fill in the blanks and suddenly the dance would start to speak. She'd wanted Marty to be there because she wanted an honest opinion, and he was the one she trusted most.

Gracie did her stretches first, switched off her sound processor, then slowly moved to the middle of the ground, closed her eyes and started to feel the music. Marty sat with his back to the wall, letting the waves of sound roll over him. She stood still at first, as if she were listening to something deep, deep inside. Closed her eyes. Felt the rhythms moving up her legs. She stood and stood and stood until she almost seemed to tip to the side. She took a step. Swayed her arms.

There didn't seem to be a pattern, but it all kind of made sense. The music wasn't happy, it was a kind of – Marty hunted for the word – *regret*? Was that it?

Regretful? She wasn't there any more. Not in the way that he was. It was as if she were far away, speaking with this world through her body, but her mind seemed to be somewhere else. Marty watched her, his skin prickling. She did have a superpower. She could disappear. In this space. Dancing allowed her to imagine, and be and disappear wherever she wanted to go. She seemed totally free.

Suddenly Marty felt a tinge of something, though he wasn't sure what it was. Admiration? Yes – but it was more like envy, of the ability to be that free. That flowing. To have that space. And hope? Was that it? That somehow, far away, a tide was turning.

Gracie practised for a long time while Marty watched her. He was so spellbound that he didn't even notice the tears rolling down his cheeks.

CHAPTER TWELVE

A week later, there was a bright yellow flower on the plant. Cheery and star-shaped. Fluted but enormous, glowing in the June sun. Its leaves had covered the whole of the raised bed by now and tendrils and vines all spiky and prickly were snaking through and over each other.

'It's a pumpkin!' exclaimed Marty.

Grandad let out an enormous belly laugh.

'At last!' He clapped. 'I thought you'd never guess! But this ain't no normal pumpkin, my

boy!' he said. 'This is an Atlantic Giant Pumpkin that's going to grow to the size of a small family car!'

Gracie laughed.

'This, my dears, is going to be a pumpkin so large that they'll be able to see it for miles around. This will be the envy of everyone on this allotment and the whole city. This, my darlings, is our master plan!'

'Our master plan is that we're going to grow an enormous pumpkin?' asked Marty flatly.

Gracie giggled.

'Marty!' His grandad feigned disgust and puffed out his chest. 'Don't say it like that. We're not *just* going to grow an enormous pumpkin. It will be stupendous. Glorious. It will be the stuff of history. It will be –' he lowered his voice now and widened his eyes – 'the biggest pumpkin in the whole wide world.'

'The biggest pumpkin in the world?'

'Yes, Marty!' Grandad's whole body was quivering with excitement. 'What we're going to do,' he explained, 'is let it set fruit, and when it does we'll chop off every single one except the biggest and the strongest and the healthiest. We'll pick one and put all our efforts into it.

103

Treat it like a king. Feed it till it's obese, massage it with oils, give it everything its little pumpkiny heart could desire and then, only THEN, will we start to have some fun! You see, growing the pumpkin is only step one . . .'

His eyes were shining now.

'It's step two I am really interested in . . .'

'What? What's step two?' asked Gracie, leaning in.

Grandad leaned even closer . . .

'Step two is the most glorious thing you've ever heard. Step two will blow your tiny little minds. Step two . . . will be le-gen-dar-y . . .'

Gracie was studying him, her face getting closer and closer to his, spellbound.

'And step two will be . . . ?' she prompted.

She waited for an answer. Grandad held the drama a little longer until he confided . . .

'*That*, my kiddos, is a surprise . . .'

'Oh my goodness, Grandad! You can't do this!' said Marty, exasperated.

Gracie's shoulders dropped in disappointment.

'. . . but, suffice to say, it's going to be spectacularous!'

Marty rolled his eyes.

'You have to dream big, kiddies! Dream big! Now, come on!'

The allotment was bursting out all over now. Buds and saplings, sprouting bulbs and creeping tendrils. It was as if everything was setting out its plans for summer. Feeling its own potential.

'Well, stop standing around gawping! We've got work to do!'

Grandad led them to the back of the shed where he had a barrel. He gestured to Marty and Gracie to look in. Marty then noticed the smell. Gracie took one look before starting to retch.

'Oh my God!' she cried. 'What is that?'

'It's the basis for the pumpkin tea, my dear,' said Grandad proudly.

The barrel was three-quarters full of seaweed and slime and goodness knows what that had been stewing there for weeks since their visit to the beach.

'What it needs now is boiling up and a good stir.'

Marty and Gracie looked at each other.

'Are you *serious*?' they both exclaimed together.

'I am absolutely one hundred per cent serious!'

Gracie and Marty set about finding sticks for the fire. Grandad had an old tyre inner on which to start fires, so they piled them into that. Then they set about finding anything that could burn. Marty found the matches while Grandad rolled the barrel on its bottom edge carefully towards the fire and hoisted it up with great difficulty onto the pile, puffing heavily.

'*Woohoo!*' He exhaled, straightening up, his eyes sparkling. 'Let's brew some tea . . .'

Grandad lit the fire and they watched as the smoke rose in black columns upward before thinning out as the flames caught hold. They listened as the kindling sparked and crackled.

'It's going to take forever!' said Marty.

Grandad tapped the side of his nose before retreating to his shed to fetch his trusty bottle of petrol. He threw a glug on to the fire, making the flames jump up three metres.

'Oh my God, Grandad!' shouted Marty, feeling his face flush with heat.

'I think I've lost my eyebrows!' shouted Gracie, laughing and covering her face with her hands.

Before long, the barrel was bubbling like a cauldron. Grandad watched, rubbing his hands together in glee.

'Heh heh!' he cried. 'Come on, you two!'

It was only then that Marty and Gracie saw that Grandad had lined up some things to put into the tea. There were piles of stinging nettles, some banana skins and a bottle of yellow liquid that looked to Marty suspiciously like wee. Grandad plopped them into the barrel one by one, making weird-coloured smoke poof up like it was sending smoke signals. Then, as a pièce de la résistance, Grandad fished out a contraption from the shed. Gracie looked at Marty. Marty put his hand to his head . . .

'Oh, no . . .'

Gracie looked worried. 'What *is* that thing?'

They watched as Grandad wrestled what looked like a giant dead spider over to the barrel.

'This, my dear, is the tea stirrer 300. The new and improved version!'

He kind of threw a few of its legs over the barrel so that it was sitting on top of the liquid. Then he retreated to the shed, and after much searching and fumbling came back with a spade. He eased the spade into the barrel and slotted the handle top into the underside of the spider. He looked over at Gracie and Marty and winked. Then, he motioned to them to stand back.

'Right, then, let's see if this baby works . . .'

As he clicked the switch, the barrel shuddered. Marty grimaced and looked away. Then the spidery legs seemed to grip on to the sides of the barrel and the spade clunked against the metal.

'Oh God,' said Gracie, backing away.

'Don't worry! It'll be fine!'

The tea stirrer started to turn, slowly at first, making a whooshing sound. Then faster and faster.

The smell was brilliant. As in brilliantly, throat-scratchingly disgusting. And every now and again bubbles of a petrol-green fizz would rise to the surface and pop with rather impressive belches.

Grandad watched, his eyes shining with glee.

'Shall I turn her up?' he asked.

'No!' cried Marty, who hadn't forgotten his own mug of tea flying off sideways and spraying him with a scalding brew.

Slowly, the mixture started to boil down and get thicker. Darker. It changed in colour from a weak yellow to red to brown to an almost-black with a blue undertone. Grandad took a sniff of it as if he were a wine connoisseur checking his latest vintage. He turned off the tea stirrer 300 and scooped one of his enamel mugs into the brew and looked at it. To Marty and Gracie's horror, he started to lift the mug to his lips . . .

'Grandad! Don't!' shouted Marty.

Grandad's face creased in laughter.

'I wasn't going to! I wasn't going to!' He took a deep and satisfied sniff, then smiled. 'I think it's ready, short stuffs!'

Grandad hauled the barrel off the fire and Marty found some more wood to throw on it to keep it going for a while.

It was getting quieter on the allotment now. The sounds of doors closing. People shutting up for the evening. The barrel of pumpkin tea was steaming quietly in the evening air.

'You sure you don't need to be home for supper?' Grandad asked Gracie.

Gracie looked over at her house. It was dark. There was no one home.

'Nah, I'm all right.' She shrugged.

Grandad studied her through narrowed eyes for a moment before letting it go.

'OK, well, you asked for it . . .'

It was then that he brought a packet of lukewarm and probably highly dodgy sausages from the shed and started to grill them on a long fork over the fire. He'd swear every now and again as the fat spat back on his arm, then he'd giggle and apologize to Gracie. They all ate, burning their lips and risking food poisoning, but Marty thought those were the best sausages he'd ever tasted in his life.

CHAPTER THIRTEEN

'Marty, Marty, Marty! I tried my best to cover for you, but she's coming after you.'

It was Mr Garraway in a spectacularly tight tracksuit. He'd run along the corridor to catch up with him and was now leaning his hands on his knees breathlessly. Marty really didn't understand why someone so unfit would have such a liking for sportswear or teaching PE. He was absolutely and utterly unsuited to it. Marty had really meant to hand in some work, he really had – it was just that he hadn't quite got around to it.

'She's on your case!' Mr Garraway was hissing through his teeth now. He looked up at him.

'I'm sorry?'

'She's on your case. The big bad wolf. Boss woman.

You know . . . I told you to hand in some work. Anyway, she's caught wind of it and bing, bang, bosh she's baying for your blood . . .'

Mr Garraway obviously hadn't heard the scrape and clack of Miss James's listless heels in the corridor because by now she was standing behind him.

'I just wanted to warn you, that's all . . .'

'*Ah-hem.*'

Mr Garraway froze and turned the colour of underbaked pastry. He looked at Marty in panic.

'She's behind me, isn't she?'

Marty nodded imperceptibly.

'Yes, Mr Garraway, she is. The, erm . . . "big bad wolf", as you call her, is right here . . .'

Mr Garraway turned on his heel, feigned a wide smile and tried to style it out.

'Heh, heh, of course, when I said "big bad wolf", I wasn't referring to yourself . . .'

'Nigel, please.' Miss James dismissed him with a death stare. 'I need to talk to young Mr Marty here . . .'

Mr Garraway had started nodding and bowing as he circled Miss James gingerly and ran away up the corridor.

Miss James gestured to Marty with her head and marched him along the corridor and into her office.

She sat down and folded her fingers together on the desk and gave him a terrifyingly challenging look.

'It seems that despite some warnings you still haven't handed in any work, young man. I mean forgetfulness is one thing; blatant disobedience is another.'

She was quiet for a while. Considered him. Then she came in with a deadly blow.

'I'd like to add your mother to my list of appointments on Parents' Evening.'

Marty blanched. That was never going to happen.

'Er, well, I don't know if she'll be coming.'

Miss James raised her eyebrow.

'She works a lot,' Marty added.

'But surely she's interested in how your academic life is coming on?'

'Sure, it's just . . . she's busy, that's all.'

Miss James watched him coolly.

'Well, I'll add her to the list, and I'm sure that she'll make a great effort to come and see me.'

Marty swallowed hard.

'What if she doesn't?' he asked, without trying to sound cocky.

'Well, then, maybe I'll make an appointment with her at your home?'

Marty nodded.

'You can go . . .'

Marty had actually been looking forward to today, until he'd been cornered by Miss James. He'd got up early and cleaned a bit around the back door of the house. He'd soaked some mugs in bleach too so they were sparkling, ready for when Gracie and he had squash. Gracie was waiting for him by the bike rack. Today was the day she was coming round to Marty's. It would be the first time he'd ever had someone home and he'd really been looking forward to it. He'd been telling her a few things about Mum recently. Not the really big stuff. Just about how she wouldn't leave the house and things. Marty pushed his bike as Gracie walked, well, danced beside him.

'What's wrong?' she asked after they'd walked for a bit.

Marty shrugged. 'They want to see Mum on Parents' Evening . . .'

Gracie took this in, and started walking normally. Marty could tell she was deep in thought.

'Well, maybe she'll go?' Gracie said.

Marty had thought about this too. About how much better Mum was. How she was walking to the washing line and back. How she was still keeping on top of the mess.

'Maybe you should just ask her?'

Perhaps Gracie was right. Maybe Mum'd do it for him. She had promised. Promised to make an effort, and she was. Marty felt a little better for having told Gracie and they kept walking in silence for a while.

'I filled in my application form . . .' Gracie said at last. 'For the competition. I sent it in the post this morning . . .'

'That's great!' said Marty, genuinely pleased.

'You . . . you do realize that I'd have to change schools if I get in?'

Marty stopped in his tracks. 'Why?'

'They'd want me to train every night. I wouldn't be able to get back here every day.'

Marty gripped the handlebars of his BMX a bit tighter.

'But I'd be home every weekend.'

Marty started walking again. They walked the rest of the way in a thoughtful silence, Marty thinking how he was going to get his mum to Parents' Evening, and Gracie thinking about how much she would miss these walks if she got into the dance school. Neither of them actually noticed anything until Marty opened the back door. His eyes tried to focus, but there was just a jumbled collage of stuff. He couldn't make it make sense. He looked across at Gracie, and watched as she took in the bags of old clothes and chipped mugs and stacks of saucepans. The back room was filled. Filled completely once more with rubbish and paper and old carpet and everything else.

'I'm sorry, Marty.'

Marty's eyes found his mum eventually, kneeling on the floor among the mess.

'I can't do it. I'm not strong enough. I need my things.'

Marty could feel his heart thudding in his chest. His vision narrowed and he felt suddenly sick. His school bag slipped from his hand and then he ran. He ran and he ran, leaving Gracie looking at Marty's mum weeping on the floor.

CHAPTER FOURTEEN

'I thought I'd find you here.'

Gracie had brought Marty some breakfast from her house. She held out the jam sandwich as Marty squinted in the morning light. The allotment shed had been cold overnight. Gracie set about making some tea in silence. She didn't press Marty for any details.

'She cares more about stuff than me,' he said at last.

Gracie handed him his cup and sat down on an upturned bucket.

'Do you really think that?'

Marty's eyes were red from crying.

'She promised.'

Gracie touched his arm. Tears in her own eyes.

'I'm sorry.'

Marty pulled his arm back.

'I used to think it was normal –' he let out a bitter little laugh – 'when I was small. That everyone lived like that.'

Marty sniffed. His nose was running from having cried most of the night and his head ached.

'It's OK if you, you know . . . you don't want to be friends—'

'Don't be an idiot!' Gracie interrupted. 'Does she know you slept here?'

Marty shrugged. 'What's she going to do? Come and check?'

'She'll have phoned your grandad?'

'She'll be too busy dragging all that stuff back into the house. Once she gets like this, it's like nothing else matters . . .'

The mugs were steaming in the morning cold.

'She can totally kid herself. You'd think it'd be impossible . . . but she can kid herself that she needs those things. She lies to herself so hard that she believes it . . .'

'Maybe she does?'

'But it's so stupid!'

'Maybe we all lie to ourselves, kid ourselves that we need something or want something or can be something,' said Gracie quietly.

'But that's different!'

'Is it?' She was searching his face now. She shrugged. 'Believing things, forcing yourself to believe them, isn't always a bad thing,' she offered.

'It's stupid! We all need to accept who we are. That we can't change. If this proves anything, it proves that! And these stupid dreams of ours, they're just nonsense!'

'Don't say that!'

'Grandad and this seed, and you and your dancing! We're just kidding ourselves. The world. It doesn't care!'

Marty knew that he'd hurt her. She didn't need to say anything, but he was so angry. It was like he'd just opened the door to that room he'd shoved all his hurts into, and stuff had started tumbling out. 'People promise things they don't mean. We can't change who we are. What we've been given!'

Gracie had got up. 'I know you're angry, but—'

'Yes, I'm angry! I'm angry, all right. I'm angry that I'm

stuck, with her, in that house. And I'm angry that I don't have any choice. And I'm angry that she's so useless. And I'm angry that this is all so pointless – and I'm tired! I'm sick and tired of trying and trying and getting nowhere!'

Gracie listened, her face passive.

'You've got me, you've got your grandad.'

'Grandad?' Marty laughed. 'What does he do? He just does NOTHING! NOTHING! He just sits there and comes up with all these stupid, crazy plans and they mean NOTHING! That's why Grandma kicked him out! Because he couldn't actually come up with a plan that worked!'

There was no sound except the sound of Marty's heavy breathing. Then came a little cough behind Gracie. It was Grandad. He'd pulled off his trilby and was standing there holding it against his chest. Marty looked from Gracie's face to his grandad's and back again. He felt sick. As if all that stuff that had just come out of his mouth had an awful, nasty taste.

'Look, I'm sorry,' he said to Gracie.

She nodded. It was deadly quiet.

'I'd better go to school anyway,' Gracie said, and

turned, hoicking her bag up on her shoulder.

'Gracie, I'm sorry . . .' Marty started.

But she'd already turned and she couldn't hear him. Marty watched her walk head down through the allotments towards school. Marty stood in Grandad's gaze a moment, embarrassment burning his cheeks.

Grandad let a few moments pass.

'Well, thank goodness for that,' he said at last. 'A bit of fire. I actually thought for a moment there that your little flame had gone out.'

Marty lifted up his head.

'What?'

'I've been wondering when you'd wake up . . . like that seed. Burst open a bit. Good Lord, I thought it would never happen.' He smiled, and went to pour himself some tea.

Marty's shoulders dropped.

'It's not healthy, you know, Marty, holding everything in, holding everything back . . . That is precisely why I ain't got nothing and your mum has everything.'

'You're not angry?'

Grandad laughed.

'Of course not! I'm proud . . . Although, I don't entirely agree with you that my plans are always useless . . .' He chuckled.

Marty sat down, his eyes, his head and his whole body aching. Grandad ruffled his hair and handed him his tea.

'You know that fire you have? That's what's going to get you somewhere . . . You can't lock it all up. You've got to ride the wave. Let all those feelings go through you . . . like Gracie does when she dances . . . Don't be ashamed of what you feel. Big feelings, they turn into big dreams, brilliant things.'

'Are you sure?' Marty felt shaky, a bit newborn, squinting in the morning light.

'I'm positive. We just need to keep believing . . . Your mum, she's got some issues of her own she needs to work out. It's not her fault. She just needs time . . .'

Marty smiled a sad little smile.

'How about a day off school today? I'll write you a note tomorrow when you go back and . . . let's see if we can decide which of these pumpkins to keep.'

Marty nodded and watched as morning began to make the allotments busy. Sadiq was already watering his plants. The old lady in allotment seven was putting out bird food and making a funny squeaky noise with her lips like kissing, calling the birds to her. John Trinidad was planting in the morning light.

Grandad was right. Marty did actually feel a bit better. A bit lighter. He rubbed the back of his neck with his hand and looked at the giant pumpkin plant threading its way around the allotment. There was only one thing pressing on him, and that was how he was going to make it up to Gracie.

CHAPTER FIFTEEN

Grandad's bedsit was small. Marty was used to having no room, but Grandad's bedsit was small in a different way to Marty's house. It was just tiny. One room, half a wall, a toilet behind that and a two-ring electric cooker. He used to come for sleepovers when he was smaller, but what with the pub below it, and shouty beery people making a noise outside, Marty hardly did any sleeping. Marty watched as Grandad brushed his trilby.

Grandad had spoken to Mum on the phone. He was going to stay with Grandad for a few months. Marty had listened as Grandad explained to her that Marty was growing up now, becoming more aware of things, and that his schoolwork had started to suffer. Marty had heard her crying on the other side of the phone, but

Grandad had been firm. She needed some time to sort herself out and it wasn't fair on the boy. Marty's heart hurt as he heard his mum's muffled sobs down the line, but he tried to harden himself against it.

Gracie had been ignoring him at school. Every time he tried to catch up with her to apologize, she would slip away. Every time he tried to sneak her a note, she would bin it, unread. He had so many things to tell her. How big the pumpkin had got, how he'd moved in with Grandad and how he was really, really, really sorry. It was no use, though. It was as if she were always disappearing into thin air.

Grandad turned. 'Ready, then?'

Marty had never actually had anyone he could take to Parents' Evening before. Now, being able to skip it because nobody was interested might sound terrific, but to Marty being able to take Grandad made him feel a little bit taller.

Miss James was sitting like a stiff-looking duchess, when they went into her office. The corridors were all buzzing with parents and kids, but it was quiet in here. This was obviously where the 'problem cases' came.

'How lovely you look this evening!' Grandad said with a wink, and Marty was totally and absolutely sure that he saw Miss James blush a little. He would not have believed it had he not seen it with his own eyes. Marty watched, spellbound, as Grandad went to work.

'Before we begin, I would just like to thank you for heading up such a wonderful educational establishment.

My grandson here speaks so highly of you and all the staff.'

Miss James couldn't take her eyes off Grandad. Marty could have sworn he saw her head swell a little.

'I mean, we are lucky to have such a school so expertly run in our community.'

Miss James looked like someone who had crawled on her hands and knees in the desert of the unacknowledged for a thousand years before finally seeing an oasis of appreciation.

'Well, er, thank you—'

But before she could carry on Grandad interrupted.

'I want to talk to you about Marty here, if you don't mind . . .'

'Well, yes, of course. That's what I wanted to see you about . . .' she said, on the back foot again.

'As you know, he's very imaginative . . .'

'Well, yes . . .' She blushed slightly because she really didn't know Marty very well at all.

'And you know that he works hard.'

'Well, I wanted to ask about his homework—'

'Homework!' Grandad laughed. 'Now, now. I know you must be familiar with a certain Albert Einstein.'

'Well, yes, but—'

'Totally failed his exams. Hopeless. Couldn't do tests at all.'

'Really?'

'Absolutely. It turns out it wasn't him that wasn't right for schooling; it was just that the school wasn't right for him.'

'Yes, but . . . Mr . . . ?'

'Call me Cuthbert. I believe you're Elaine, aren't you?'

'Er, yes . . .' Miss James was completely and utterly flustered. 'I do think we should talk about Marty's attainment levels,' she said.

'Me too! I'm sure you will agree, Elaine, the true sign of intelligence is not knowledge but imagination. Guess who said that . . . ?'

Miss James looked baffled.

'Einstein again . . .' Grandad beamed at her. 'I'm so glad we're on the same page. Marty here has been doing well, and he's turning into a fine young man thanks to you! And, as we all know, you cannot judge a book by its cover, or know how the worm will turn out until it grows up.'

'Er . . . I suppose not . . .'

'Well, I'm glad we all agree.'

Grandad had stood up by now. He turned a dashing smile on Miss James. 'I'm so glad we met at last!' Then he gave her a long, studied look and drew a deep, deep breath. 'You really are an inspiration! *Such* an inspiration!'

Then he turned and dragged Marty out with him, leaving Miss James looking as if she'd been in an accident with a particularly charismatic steamroller.

Grandad and Marty picked up some chips on the way home, and decided to swing by the allotment to check on the pumpkin. Grandad lit the fire and dragged his squeaky chair outside. Marty upended an old tree stump and sat down. They ate the chips, watching the flames, their faces boiling hot and their backs freezing cold.

'Thanks for tonight,' Marty said.

Grandad smiled. 'It's OK . . .'

They listened to the wood crackle in the flames for a moment.

'It's true, you know . . . What I said about Einstein . . .'

Marty thought about this a moment.

'There's nothing we can't achieve if we can dream it . . .' Grandad added.

Marty looked doubtful.

Grandad looked at him. 'So, you want to know what the big plan is?'

Marty looked up. Grandad had shuffled to the end of his chair.

'Are you actually going to tell me this time?'

'I think it's time . . .' Grandad said, his eyes suddenly becoming animated. He leaned closer to Marty. Looked around. Made sure there was no one listening. Not that there was anyone on the allotments at this time of night except for a few owls.

'What are we going to do, Grandad?'

Grandad paused dramatically, fixed Marty with a wonderful smile and said . . .

'We're going to Paris . . .'

'What?' exclaimed Marty. 'You won the lottery or something?'

'Nope! It's an absolutely delicious plan, Marty! We're not going by plane . . .'

'Sorry, Grandad, I don't get it . . .'

Grandad took his time, enjoying the expressions on Marty's face.

'We are going to grow this pumpkin until it's HUGE.' His eyes were smiling now. 'And then, when it's as big as it can be, we'll scoop out the bits in the middle, fit an outboard engine on it, add a sail and off we go!'

Marty didn't quite know what Grandad had expected, a round of applause or what, but he just looked at him, mouth agape.

'We're going to sail to Paris in a pumpkin?'

'Yes, we are! And before you think it's a bonkers idea, I worked it all out! They're buoyant. I've almost finished tinkering with that old outboard engine; all we need now is a good headwind and we'll be there!'

Marty started to laugh. Laugh and laugh. It started with a smile and then a giggle and a chuckle and a snort until it was full-on, full-throttle laughing. He hadn't actually laughed like that since he was a kid.

Grandad watched his face, searching for a reaction other than laughter. When Marty finally stopped, tears rolling down his face, Grandad scratched his head, leaning closer to Marty.

'So? What do you think?'

Marty looked at him. He was absolutely serious.

'Grandad, I think you're mad!'

Grandad looked a little crestfallen.

'I mean, it doesn't make sense. It's actually mad!'

Grandad considered this.

'I'd rather be mad, Marty, my boy, than boring. Just think of it! You. Me. That gorgeous pumpkin boat and the big blue sea.'

'But it's impossible!'

'It isn't! Look at it! It's already a great-looking pumpkin! We just need to swell it a bit. Then we'll need some expanding foam, a sail, some rope and some help from Colin the milkman. But, Marty, I'm absolutely sure we could do it!'

Marty looked confused. Grandad took his hand.

'Listen to me, Marty. I know you've . . . Things haven't been easy. People have let you down, but you can't lose your dreams; you can't stop believing that anything is possible. And if I can achieve anything in this life I'll prove that to you . . .'

Marty tried not to cry. It was really hard these days.

It was like there were all these tears just bubbling under the surface and all they needed was the gentlest of nudges and – *whoosh* – they might all come tumbling out.

'It's going to be brilliant, Marty! Trust me.'

Marty looked at him, his face lit up by the fire, and he wanted, more than anything, to trust him with all his heart.

CHAPTER SIXTEEN

G racie had sat on her bed thinking about what Marty had said every night for a week. Sometimes, she'd move over to the window and watch as Marty and his grandad worked on the allotment. She had really wanted to go over. She knew he hadn't meant what he'd said, that he'd been angry, but she was angry now too. She'd managed to avoid him in school and had kept the light off at home even though she was there in case he'd come over from the allotment.

Today she'd waited until everyone had left the school – the teachers who worked late and the cleaners – and when the school was entirely empty she'd sat on the grass and slipped off her shoes and socks. She'd placed her phone to the whispering wall and closed her eyes.

She'd concentrated, but it was as if there was nothing there. Well, perhaps not nothing, but she was angry inside. Scowling. She was shocked for a moment. Gracie opened her eyes and closed them and tried again. She waited for her arms and her legs to take their cue from the music, but again nothing happened. She opened her eyes. Furious.

Then she'd walked home. All the way. Her feet stomping on the pavement until she walked up the garden path and slammed the door behind her. It wasn't as if she hadn't been through tough things before. It wasn't as if she hadn't been hurt by things people had said. She just felt foolish. Embarrassed. Like she'd shown Marty this side of her and he'd thrown it back in her face.

'Blimey, you OK?'

It was her dad. She hadn't expected him to be home.

'Looks like you're about to murder someone . . .'

He was standing there in a fresh shirt and jeans, obviously preparing for a night out.

'It's not funny, Dad.'

She turned to walk upstairs, out of his way.

'Gracie? What's wrong?'

136

She turned back to face him.

'Nothing. OK? I'm fine. I'm absolutely fine.'

She thought of telling him. She really wanted to sometimes, but she just didn't know where she'd start with this whole mess.

'You know you can talk to me, don't you?'

'Can I?'

He looked hurt by that. He walked towards her.

'Of course you can. You look so upset.'

Gracie was upset. She was tired and upset and she felt really silly. Her dad was looking at her now.

'It's just . . .' she started.

'It's just what?' he asked.

It was then that his mobile rang. Gracie looked at the table. Willing him not to pick it up. He did, of course. Then she thought he'd just check the number and put it down again, but he didn't. He looked flustered, then guilty. 'You don't mind if I quickly get this, do you?' he said, and answered it anyway.

Gracie watched him as he started talking business with someone she didn't know. She kicked off her shoes, and turned to climb the stairs to her bedroom. By the time he had started looking for her again, she had locked herself in the bathroom and run the taps so he would think she was having a bath. Then she'd sat on the edge of the tub waiting for him to leave before eventually feeling the vibration of the front door shutting heavily through her bare feet.

CHAPTER SEVENTEEN

S everal weeks had gone by. It was now mid-July and the pumpkin had stopped growing. Despite being fed regularly with the seaweed tea and watered several times a day, its belly stubbornly refused to swell. It had swollen from the size of a football to the size of a large beach ball, but now it had somehow stalled. As if it had thought to itself, *That's quite enough, thank you; that's me done.*

Grandad had been measuring it with a measuring tape every day and had become quieter and quieter and more preoccupied. Marty had watched him, unable to offer him any ideas, and then Grandad did something very surprising. Something very surprising indeed. Something Marty had never thought he'd do in a million years. He called a meeting. An allotment meeting. He spread some old paint pots here and there for people to sit on, and lit a fire. He propped up an old piece of board and used the tea stirrer 300 as an easel. Over the board, he spread the map from the shed wall. Marty had absolutely no idea what he was doing or what the plan was.

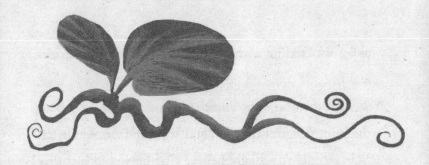

Marty watched as Sadiq and John, the lady from allotment number seven whose name no one knew, Colin the milkman and a few others all came over. They were talking among themselves, wondering aloud what on earth was going on, when Grandad whacked an empty tin bucket with a spoon and called the meeting to order. He cleared his throat, and for once in Marty's life he was sure he saw some uncertainty in Grandad's eyes. Marty took a seat nearest the pumpkin and waited.

'Right, you've been called here in the strictest confidence because Marty and I, well, we need your help.'

Everyone looked at each other.

'I've tried everything, but I just can't get that pumpkin to grow . . .'

John scratched his head. 'You've called us here for tips on how to grow that pumpkin?'

'Yes,' admitted Grandad, pulling at his collar a little

as he was feeling so hot. 'But it's for a very particular reason . . .'

And then he went on to tell them *everything*. About the pumpkin and the plan and Paris and the whole lot. Marty couldn't actually believe that he would just dive in and tell them like that. There was something so risky about it. So bold and crazy that it felt like madness.

'We'll have four days of fresh pumpkin. I mean, if you've ever seen those left over after Halloween hanging about on walls, you know they last ages,' Grandad continued. He pulled a battered old *Tide Table* book out of his shirt pocket and started to rifle in it.

'I've worked it out. There's a gap, four days at the end of August. If we leave here on the twenty-seventh of August, we'll catch favourable tides all the way there and back.'

His hands were trembling as he stuffed the *Tide Table* book back into his pocket and proceeded to extend an antenna that he'd taken off an old radio to its full length and use it to point at the map.

'If we could get the pumpkin to Southampton, it's one hundred and twenty-seven nautical miles to Le Havre.'

The audience followed his pointer across the map over the expanse of emptiness between England and France.

'I reckon, full tilt, we could get that engine going at around twenty-five knots. With a good tailwind behind us, that's . . .' Grandad screwed up his face in calculation.

'Four hours . . .' Colin offered.

'Exactly. Four hours.'

Grandad was getting excited now; Marty could feel it. He watched as Grandad jotted down the numbers on the map with a half-chewed pencil from behind his ear. 'That's a trifling, piffling little distance; we could do that easily! Stop over at Le Havre for the night here . . . and boom! The next morning, we're off up the Seine . . .'

Sadiq scratched his head. Marty listened as the assembled company tried to get their heads round Grandad's plan.

'You'll go up the Seine?' said Sadiq.

Grandad looked at Sadiq as if he were mad.

'Of course!' he said, making it sound so simple. 'We'll sail up it. It's around ninety-six miles. Start first thing. The Seine is tidal. It'll practically sweep us into the city by mid-morning.'

'Into Paris?' Colin looked up.

'Yes. Paris,' said Grandad.

Marty laughed.

'Let me get this straight, my lovelies,' said Colin carefully. 'You are going to grow this pumpkin until it's massive, carve it out, stick an old engine on it and then you're just going to casually sail into the city of Paris in a pumpkin?'

Grandad sat back and rubbed his belly in excitement.

'Absolutely! The only problem we have is that the pumpkin has stalled. We're going to need it to be the size of a family car in six weeks' time, and at the moment that is looking increasingly unlikely.'

Colin looked on in bewilderment. Marty could feel them catching Grandad's excitement. He could feel their hearts and heads start to fill up with the idea. The lady from allotment seven started giggling and everyone started smiling at each other. Marty's stomach was in knots as he waited for one of them to react.

'Well, we'll have to think of something!' said Colin. 'I think that's the best thing I've ever heard!'

Marty could have kissed him.

And then the others started clapping. Grandad looked over their heads at Marty and winked.

After a quick cup of tea, which they had to drink in shifts because there weren't enough mugs to go round, they huddled around the fire and started to share suggestions.

'Have you tried eggshells?' asked Sadiq.

Grandad nodded.

'Beer?' asked John.

'We've tried that too . . .'

Now that everyone knew the importance of getting this thing as big as possible, they started racking their brains about how to do it. The seaweed tea had worked up to a point, but it seemed to need something extra. Something that would get it going again.

'Have you tried reading to it?' came a quiet voice. It was the lady from allotment number seven. 'Some people swear by talking to plants.'

Grandad shook his head. 'It's worth a try.' He jotted it down.

'How about bird manure?' It was Colin this time.

'I have bird manure,' said the lady from number seven again.

Marty collected the mugs and went to make another round of tea. He'd never seen such a buzz at the allotment. It was like there was a little electricity in the air. A sense of shared adventure. Everyone in on the plan and bound together in secrecy. Every time he thought about Grandad's adventure, his stomach would quiver. His insides would jiggle a bit. He'd kind of got used to the deadening dimness of Mum's house, but thinking of the sea made him feel giddy. He just wished Gracie was with him so he could talk to her about it. He imagined telling her in his head. The look on her face. What she would say.

He looked over at her house – there was no life there. No movement. Marty had thought of a hundred ways to say sorry, but none of them actually felt right, so in the end he'd sketched out the idea for the boat on a piece of paper as well as the distance to Paris and a wobbly picture of the Eiffel Tower and, as he didn't know what else to do, he found Gracie's bag at lunchtime, hanging on her hook, and slipped it in there and skulked away. But days had passed by now and he'd heard nothing. He boiled the kettle and looked back towards the huddled bunch in front of the fire and wished with all his heart that she was there.

CHAPTER EIGHTEEN

Sadiq had lent Grandad his water butt so that they could carry water to the pumpkin more easily. John Trinidad had started sprinkling some mysterious powder on to the roots of the pumpkin, and he'd stand there willing it to grow. The lady from allotment seven had started to read it poetry. She began with the Romantics, worked her way through Keats and Coleridge, before deciding that, actually, the pumpkin may like something a little bit more modern. Since then she'd been trying Dylan Thomas, Maya Angelou and Benjamin Zephaniah, but to no avail. Colin the milkman had scooped up bucketfuls of bird poo and had scattered it about, hoping it might make a little difference. A week had gone by, but the pumpkin still sat there stubbornly, the same size.

Grandad, however, had tried to keep things as cheerful as ever and, as it was the first proper warm day of summer, he had dragged the rickety table from the shed into the open and set about tinkering with the outboard engine until his fingers and clothes were covered in oil. It was as if by keeping on with his plan he was keeping the dream alive.

Marty had kept himself busy all day, watering and feeding the pumpkin and doing odd jobs around the allotments. He'd watched over Grandad's shoulder as he tweaked the engine and laughed as Grandad fired it up, so that it blew plumes of black smoke everywhere until they both nearly choked.

It was getting darker now, and this was Marty's favourite time at the allotments. The bees would hum lazily and you could just feel everything and every plant just breathe out for the night. Relax. The daisies would close up their petals for the evening and the other flowers would release their scents. The light would soften too and the yellow light of day would mellow to peach and then blue and then a deep, rich navy.

Marty made his grandad some tea and lit the fire. He

watched as the sparks blew upward with the wind for a while. He'd done some schoolwork, as Mr Garraway had suggested. Marty had brought it to the allotment and done it while his grandad pottered. Colin the milkman had helped a little. He was good at maths, and Sadiq was the guy to help with languages. Marty had done a lot in a very short period of time and hoped that it would be enough to tide him over until the end of the summer term in a couple of weeks. It all felt a little more important now. It was the way Mr Garraway had explained it, that he had a brain and it was his responsibility to see where it would go.

Marty listened as the flames grew stronger, casting a soft amber light on to everything. It was getting darker now and Marty looked over at the pumpkin. It seemed to be almost glowing in the firelight. It was an illusion, of course, but there was something about its orange skin that made it look molten, as if it had been poured from a furnace. He got up, leaving the fire's warmth behind. He went to sit next to it.

Getting the pumpkin to the size of a small car by the end of summer still felt impossible. They'd need it to be big enough to fit Marty and Grandad comfortably, and tall enough not to sit too low in the water. They'd need the skin to be thick enough to withstand the water and the waves, and for the walls of the pumpkin to be strong enough to withstand any rough weather. It was a big, *big* ask. Marty looked at the pumpkin. Its skin was a deep and shocking orange.

He sat beside it for a moment before pulling out the little statue of the Eiffel Tower from his pocket. It was only a few centimetres high. Made of a silver metal, which by now had chipped here and there. He turned it in his fingers and watched as it glinted in the warm light. It felt so familiar in his hands. He knew every angle. Every curve.

His father had been born in Paris. That was one of the very few things he knew about him. In Marty's mind, he could barely separate the two. The Eiffel Tower and Dad. When he was small, he remembered asking him where the sun went at night, or how many stars there were, but now that he was growing up he had different kinds of questions. Marty continued to turn the tower over in his fingers and thought of his father out there in the world.

'Grandad said we're going to sail in you,' he whispered to the pumpkin. 'I think it's absolutely bonkers, but he says that you're going to take us to see the Eiffel Tower.'

Marty listened. There was nothing but the sound of Grandad tinkering and the crackle of the fire.

'I know it's not true, but . . .' Marty smiled wistfully. 'There's a part of me that wishes it was . . .'

Marty looked over at Grandad, who was finishing up fiddling with the engine, so Marty got to his feet and started to walk over to him to help him clear away his tools. It was late, and they needed to get home.

Behind him, the pumpkin creaked, its skin luminous in the firelight. Its tendrils curled a little as its rotund body swelled and groaned. It expanded. Pushing out its waist. It became bigger and bigger until it was the size of a lorry tyre. By the time Marty and Grandad closed the gate on their way home, it sat resplendent, like a glorious setting sun, glowing on the rich soil.

CHAPTER NINETEEN

Marty couldn't believe his eyes. Grandad stood next to him in wonder, then took off his hat and scratched his head.

'What on earth did you give it last night, Marty?'

Marty could feel his heart beating in his chest. His mouth was dry.

'I don't know . . . I . . .'

'But it's doubled in size, overnight?'

Marty looked at it in confusion.

'I . . . I . . . I gave it some tea . . . like you told me to . . . and I . . .'

The pumpkin's sides were spilling out over the raised bed. Like a large bottom on a narrow train seat.

'But . . . but it doesn't make sense?' Grandad stood

wide-eyed. 'I mean, I know . . . I know the tea is helping, the bananas and the wee . . .'

'Oh my God, Grandad – it was *wee*?'

'Of course it was,' said Grandad distractedly, 'but I've never known a pumpkin to double in size overnight.'

Marty racked his brains.

'I gave it some tea and then . . .' Marty tried to think. He'd been thinking about Gracie; he remembered that. He remembered talking to it . . . saying that he wished . . . Marty's mouth dropped open.

Grandad looked at him. 'What? What is it, Marty?'

'I . . . I was talking to it . . . and . . .'

He felt faint. He did feel weird whenever he was around the pumpkin. He felt things. He felt its energy. He felt something trembling inside him. He felt alive . . .

'What, Marty? Tell me . . .'

'I was talking to it . . . and . . .'

It made no sense at all, but somehow Marty knew it was true. Then Marty set off at a run.

'Marty!' he could hear his grandad shout behind him.

Marty shouted back over his shoulder. 'I'll be back in two minutes!'

He ran across the allotments, jumping over netting and wire and plants, rousing shouts of 'Oi! What are you doing?' and 'Marty, is that you?' everywhere. He ran in a straight line towards Gracie's house and jumped over the hedge. He ran up the concrete path and prayed that Gracie was home. He opened the door and ran straight in.

'Gracie? GRACIE!'

His voice echoed in the tiled space.

'Gracie? You here?'

He heard footsteps, then saw Gracie coming down the stairs. She stopped halfway. She looked at him standing there, his muddy shoes making a mess all over the pristine floor.

'You've got to come with me . . .'

'What on earth are you doing here, Marty?'

Marty's chest was still heaving.

'Come on . . . come with me . . .'

Gracie shook her head.

'I'm not talking to you, remember?' She crossed her arms.

'Look, I know I messed up. I know I was horrible.

None of that matters now. Please come with me?'

Gracie's resolve was wavering. She'd never actually seen him like this before. His cheeks were bright red and his eyes were shining. She'd never actually seen him so full of energy. He was holding his hand out to her now.

'Come on . . .'

Gracie found herself pulling on her boots despite herself and following him out of the front door, which he'd left wide open.

She ran after him until they reached the allotment where Grandad was still looking at the enormous pumpkin and scratching his head.

'Talk to it,' said Marty breathlessly.

Gracie looked at him. 'What?'

'Tell it . . . tell it your dreams . . .'

'Are you nuts? Have you actually gone and lost it this time?'

'No, listen to me.' Marty's face was serious now.

'You have to tell it . . . your wishes . . . your dreams . . . I don't know anyone with bigger dreams than you.'

Even Grandad was looking confused by now.

Marty was looking at Gracie. Waiting for her to say something.

'Go on . . .'

Gracie shook her head. 'No.'

'Gracie, please. Tell it about your competition. About how you want to be a dancer.'

Gracie looked worried now.

'It can't happen. You said so yourself . . . It was a stupid dream.'

Marty shook his head.

'I was wrong, Gracie. I was so utterly and completely wrong. It is possible . . .'

He walked towards her and took both her hands.

'You can be a brilliant dancer. You will smash this competition and I . . . Grandad and I will sail to Paris in that pumpkin . . .'

Gracie looked at him. He looked positively glowing.

'You've got to trust me! Just tell it. Believe it. I promise you . . . it'll be brilliant.'

There was something in his eyes that made Gracie nod. She turned, nodded again and walked towards the pumpkin. She looked back uncertainly at Marty and his grandad. Swallowed down hard.

The pumpkin sat, beautiful and round, in the warm sun.

'I . . . I dream of being a dancer . . .'

Her voice was small. Marty watched carefully. There was no movement.

'I want to be a dancer. I want to dance in this competition,' she went on.

And then she felt stupid. Self-conscious. Talking to a pumpkin in the middle of the allotment. 'This is stupid! Nothing's happening!'

Marty shook his head. Nothing was happening. Nothing was happening at all. The pumpkin sat immovable. His face fell. Gracie was looking at him now, her face full of confusion and embarrassment.

'I can't believe you made me do that.' Gracie looked as if she were about to cry when there was a loud groan behind her.

Marty looked over. The creaking came again. Gracie turned back slowly to look at the pumpkin. A shudder now, and then another. The pumpkin was growing. Right in front of their eyes. It was swelling. Getting fatter.

Grandad reached up to his head and slowly took his hat off in reverence. They watched as the pumpkin plumped itself out. Exhaled. Let it all hang out. They watched and waited and then, with creaks and shudders, it stopped.

Grandad studied the pumpkin in wonder. He tried speaking. Nothing came out. He tried again. Eventually, the words came from somewhere . . .

'I have never, ever seen anything so utterly and wonderfully more brilliant!'

Marty laughed. He laughed and laughed. He jumped up and whooped.

'It can hear us!' he shouted.

Gracie and Marty and Grandad started to dance around hand in hand, and the pumpkin just sat there listening and growing and knowing.

When they'd all stopped dancing around, Grandad straightened out his waistcoat and told Gracie the plan. Marty watched her as it dawned on her what a bonkers thing they were about to do. Ever since this boat thing had started, he'd really wanted to tell his mum, but telling Gracie about it was the next best thing.

'So,' said Grandad expectantly, 'what do you think?'

Gracie looked at him. 'I think it's absolutely and brilliantly bonkers!'

Grandad grinned broadly. 'Are you in?'

Marty looked at her.

'I am one hundred per cent and absolutely IN!'

'Ha ha!' Grandad said in glee. 'I knew you would be. I'm almost done on the engine. We'll just need to carve a space for it in the bottom of the pumpkin after we scoop it all out and then we'll wedge that thing in there and fill in the gaps with expanding foam. It's marvellous stuff. We'll need a mast, of course. I've an old outside umbrella stick here somewhere and a sail. We'll need some life jackets . . .'

'My dad,' said Gracie, 'he started dinghy sailing once. We've got a pile of life jackets in the garage.'

'Brilliant!' exclaimed Grandad. 'Perfectly brilliant. We're talking four days. One over to Le Havre. One up the Seine and into Paris. And two back. So we'll need food, water.'

'And maybe a mobile phone?' asked Gracie. 'I've got one of those.'

160

Grandad nodded, clearly liking the way she was thinking . . .

'Plastic bags to put things in to keep them dry,' he added.

'And a bucket in case we need to bail out,' suggested Gracie.

'Good thinking, Batman, yes!' Grandad agreed.

'When is all this happening?' asked Gracie.

Grandad sucked in a breath between his teeth. 'Well, we'll need the pumpkin to grow . . .'

'But we know how to make it grow now . . .' Marty chipped in.

'Yes, but we're going to need a lot of dreams and wishes,' replied Grandad.

'Where are we going to find those?' asked Marty.

Grandad took him by the shoulders. 'The people of this town, they're full of dreams. Things they want and wish for!' Grandad's face was alive. He looked in Marty's eyes. 'If we can find them, and make it grow . . . we're on our way!'

'When are we going?' asked Gracie.

'The twenty-seventh of August! Mark it in your diary, young lady!'

'Wait, but my audition's in London the day before,' said Gracie.

'That's OK. You can get there and back in a day, no problem,' answered Grandad, grinning. 'Plus, it'll be good to get it under your belt before we set off.'

Gracie nodded in agreement as Grandad screwed up his face in concentration.

'Two days there, two days back, and we'll be home on the . . .'

'Mum's birthday,' answered Marty, suddenly still.

Grandad smiled at him. 'Well, isn't that poetic. The thirtieth? Of course it is. Well, that's just meant to be, then.'

Marty watched as Grandad clapped his hands.

'What we're missing is some sailcloth for that sail . . .'

Gracie looked stumped.

'I know where we can find some,' Marty chimed in. 'And strong rope.'

He knew exactly where there was a fold of sailcloth and a coil of white rope; they were in the old washing machine in Marty's back garden outside the back room window. He knew precisely where they were, but that, of course, would mean going back home . . .

CHAPTER TWENTY

Gracie had asked Mr Philpott the geography teacher around two hundred and twenty-six questions about tides and shipping lanes. Mr Philpott was delighted as you couldn't usually hear anything in his class except the sound of children snoring. As it was the last day of school before the summer holidays, he'd brought in a game of Capital City Bingo to play, and all the other kids were glad of Gracie's distraction so they could just go off into their summer holiday plans in their heads.

Marty and Gracie had been at the deserted library all lunchtime, and had done some research on the school computer. As long as the 'boat' was seaworthy, there was nothing in the law to stop them. They smiled at each other when they read this and, as they had a free lesson after lunch, they had the whole place to themselves for another hour.

They found out that rubbing duck fat on the bottom of the pumpkin would protect it from the salt in the sea. Marty was glad when Gracie also pointed out that sharks weren't vegetarians, so it was looking good on the old 'fish eating the boat' scenario too. The more they talked about it, the more real it began to seem. Gracie and Marty sat in the echoing library, thinking, their minds whirring.

'Are you going to tell your mum?' Gracie asked, biting her bottom lip, not wanting to intrude.

Marty shook his head. 'I thought about it . . . but then . . . what difference would it make? I'm going to be with Grandad . . .'

'Fair enough.'

'What about your dad?' Marty asked.

Gracie looked down. 'I don't know. I suppose I'll have to tell him. It'll be in the holidays and I'll never get away with saying it's a school trip or anything.'

'Do you want Grandad to talk to your dad?'

Gracie laughed. 'God no!' She shrugged. 'I'll work it out. Nearer the time . . .'

They sat in silence a moment.

'You're really lucky, you know, Marty . . .'

Now, Marty would describe himself in a lot of different ways, but 'lucky' wasn't one of them.

'You think?'

'Your family, they're not boring.'

Marty laughed out loud.

'Ha! Well, you're right there!'

'But you don't realize how lucky you are . . . Mine, they're . . .' Gracie's voice trailed off.

Marty's face fell. There was real pain in her eyes.

'They had to fight so much for me when I was small . . . with doctors . . . speech therapy . . . It's like fighting for me was the only thing Mum and Dad had in common. The only thing that held them together. By the time I got a little older and didn't need them so much, they realized they had nothing to say to each other . . . and since they'd actually never really talked to *me* . . . everything just kind of went quiet . . .'

Marty listened.

'It's just . . . I miss them . . .'

The silence around them deepened somehow.

'I really miss both of them.'

'I miss my dad too sometimes,' Marty confided, 'even though I never really knew him . . .'

'And I miss my dad, even though I live with him.'

They smiled at each other sadly.

'Can I just ask . . . I mean, you don't have to tell me or anything,' said Gracie, 'but why Paris? Why have you always wanted to go there?'

Marty slipped his hand into his pocket, and checked the model was there as he did unconsciously several times a day.

'My dad grew up there,' he explained. 'He used to tell me stories about the place, how wonderful it was . . .'

'And is he there now?' Gracie asked, studying him.

Marty tried to not look at her.

'I don't know,' he said.

'Imagine if we bumped into him! How weird would that be?'

Marty smiled and tried to pretend that he hadn't thought of that too . . .

'I don't know . . .' He ran out of words.

They sat in silence for a moment, aware of the

other kids playing outside.

'The one thing I do know, though,' said Marty after a while, 'is it's your dad that's missing out. On your dancing. And you're going to ace this competition, and after that you and me and Grandad are going to sail that pumpkin to Paris if it's the last thing we do!'

Gracie smiled at him.

'I like this new you . . .' she said.

'You know what?' He paused. 'I think I do too.'

All the kids spilt out of the school gates, loud and lairy. There was a certain energy that came with six hundred children being let off the hook for six weeks. You could taste it in the air. Marty always used to watch their faces as he unchained his bike at the end of term. There were the lucky ones, whose mums had brought them a picnic as a nice start to the summer holidays and were waiting for them, ready to walk to the park, a ball tucked under their arms. Then there were the rich ones, whose parents were waiting in their four-by-fours ready to drive straight for the airport. They would be sitting on a beach in Portugal by the next morning. Then there were the kids being picked up by grandparents, sentenced to six weeks of being taken here and there because their parents couldn't get the time off work or some wally of a boss wouldn't let them change their shift patterns. And then there were the ones like Marty. Slow to leave the school. Knowing that the next six weeks were going to be, well, difficult. Maybe boring. That they might get hungry. That there would be no routine. Nothing really to look forward to. This was the first year Marty hadn't felt that way and his heart ached for the ones who did.

Gracie was waiting for him by the gates and they walked off in the direction of the allotments together. Marty heard the bikes behind them. He nudged Gracie, who turned. She rolled her eyes to see some of the new-trainer kids following them.

'Take no notice,' she whispered.

'Oi! Stinkfest!'

'Just leave us alone, Gerry,' Marty said over his shoulder.

'Going anywhere nice over the summer?'

Marty ignored him. If only he knew!

'You and your girlfriend going to be snogging or what?'

Marty blushed deep scarlet at this. He hoped that Gracie hadn't caught what he said.

'Leave us alone . . .' Marty said again.

'Or what?'

It was inevitable really. There was always an 'Or what?' with these kids.

Marty snapped. Turned.

'Or I'll tell all your friends here how you were snivelling under your mummy's arm when I hit you on the nose . . .'

Some of the other kids behind him laughed. It was Gerry's turn to blush. Then there was a tense stand-off. Marty wasn't sure what was going to happen, to be honest, but he thought he may as well stand his ground.

'Whatever . . .' Gerry said at last, cocking his head to the side. Then he fixed Marty with a spiteful look. 'Heard you've got a new hobby . . . Down the allotment . . .'

Marty didn't know that he knew about this, but Marty walked back this way every day and Gerry must've seen him there.

'What of it?'

'Sounds like *smashing* fun . . .'

The way he emphasized 'smashing' made Marty's blood run cold.

'What did you say?'

'Nothing.' Gerry smirked and pushed past Marty and Gracie, and the others followed, one of them spitting a big gob of snot down on Marty's trainers.

Marty watched them go.

'They know about the pumpkin . . .' said Marty.

Gracie looked troubled too. 'How?'

Marty shrugged. People must have been talking about it.

'I suppose it's not every day you get someone growing a pumpkin that big . . .'

The thought of something happening to it made Marty feel sick.

'Come on,' Gracie said. 'We'll just have to tell your grandad . . .'

CHAPTER TWENTY-ONE

B y the middle of summer, Marty had taken to sleeping in the allotment shed in a sleeping bag in order to keep an eye on the pumpkin. Grandad would sometimes join him if his back wasn't playing up too much. Every night before going to sleep, Marty would signal to Gracie with his torch that he was OK. Gracie would stand at her bedroom window and flash her torch back in a secret code. Marty would sleep well at night, having spent all day tending the pumpkin and hanging out in the fresh air, but he sometimes woke in a cold sweat, convinced he'd heard the new-trainer gang hanging about. Gracie tried to convince him that they'd forgotten all about it now that the summer holidays were in full swing and that they were probably somewhere else making

some other poor kid's life a misery.

The pumpkin was now enormous. It filled the seed bed completely and Grandad had had to build a scaffold around its edges with planks. Grandad had been whispering his wishes to it, and so had the lady from allotment seven. Sadiq had had a quiet word, and John Trinidad had been whispering to it for *hours*. The only one who hadn't quite come up with a wish yet was Colin the milkman. With every wish, it had swelled, round and fat, gourdy and bumpy on the bottom. It was a truly magnificent sight.

And the bigger it got, the bigger the buzz about the pumpkin became. People started to visit. First, it was just random people passing by that stopped to gawp at it and take a picture with it, but soon, as word spread, more people came. Grandad had watched them come, one after another, and had put a bucket nearby so he could charge them fifty pence each. The money would come in handy, of course, when they were buying supplies to take with them to Paris.

Then, one day, a thin, jittery man turned up in a grey trench coat, a camera hanging round his neck and a pen stuffed behind his ear. He stood, looking at the pumpkin, hands on his hips.

'You OK?' Grandad asked.

'Mornin', sir,' he replied. 'This 'ere your pumpkin?'

Grandad took off his hat and studied him a moment. 'Maybe . . .'

Grandad had owed enough money to random people over his lifetime not to admit who he was immediately.

The man smiled. 'Gavin Reading, *Nightly Gazette*.' He took a card from his coat pocket and handed it to Grandad.

Marty was picking peas and shelling them, popping them into his mouth like sweets. He moved closer in order to listen.

'We'd like to do a little feature. In the paper. Nothing fancy. Picture of this here pumpkin and you, if that'd be all right?'

Grandad cocked his head.

'It might be, if the price was right . . .'

The man laughed. 'We're only the local paper . . .'

Grandad started walking back to the shed, his back to him.

174

'All right . . . all right, mate,' he conceded. 'I'm sure we could sort out a couple of quid . . .'

Grandad smiled, winked at Marty before turning round.

'Especially if you give our readers some of your secrets . . .' The man was scratching his head by now. 'Tell me, how did you get it to grow so big?'

'Ah,' Grandad said, 'those are very big secrets . . .'

The man looked genuinely intrigued. 'You see, our readers, they like to get the inside info . . . the truth . . .'

'Well,' said Grandad. 'If the price is right, we can always talk truths . . .'

Marty was still shelling peas when Gracie appeared beside him.

'What's happening?' she asked.

'I'm watching a master at work,' Marty whispered back.

'Please, step into my office . . .' said Grandad, gesturing to the shed. Then he winked at Marty and Gracie again and followed the journalist inside.

Marty strained to listen at the half-open window round the back of the shed.

'What's he doing?' Gracie whispered.

'I reckon he's turning a situation to his advantage.'

Marty pressed his ear up against the glass and, sure enough, Grandad was telling Gavin Reading that the pumpkin was actually a wishing pumpkin. That it grew on people's dreams. Marty could see the smudgy outline of the man scribbling furiously. He could tell that the journalist was as captivated as Miss James had been at school.

By the time they left the shed, the man had promised to pay Grandad one hundred pounds for the story, and he took a photo of Grandad, Marty and Gracie grinning by the giant pumpkin.

'Thanks for that . . .' the journalist said, feeling like he'd got the scoop of the century.

'That's OK . . .' Grandad grinned.

'By the way,' he said, putting the pencil back behind his ear, 'what are you going to do with it when it's stopped growing? Pie? Soup?'

'Ah!' Grandad exclaimed, walking towards him and placing his arm round his shoulders. 'I thought you'd never ask . . .'

The man looked twitchy now as Grandad walked him towards the allotment gate.

'We have something splendid planned. Something stupendous. Something that will blow your mind!'

You could almost see the man quivering with excitement and the promise of a promotion from his boss.

'You come back here early doors on the twenty-seventh of August and I promise you a story that will wake up the whole world!'

He was nodding, hanging on every word.

'I will . . .'

'And we won't talk to anyone else. They'll be fighting for the story, but you, my man, will be the one we'll talk to . . .'

'OK . . .'

'And remember to bring your camera!'

'I will!'

He almost fell out through the gate as he was still watching Grandad's face, like a little bird entranced by a worm in the beak of its daddy bird.

'Take care now!' said Grandad.

The journalist nodded and off he went.

CHAPTER TWENTY-TWO

'Look at this!'

Gracie spread the newspaper out on the table in the shed. Grandad sucked the air through his teeth and gave a deep and hearty belly laugh.

'It's super!'

The pumpkin did actually look enormous in the photo; it was something about the angle of the shot.

Marty smiled and for a moment wondered whether his mum would see this. They didn't get a paper delivered, but he wondered if someone would tell her. I mean, he'd never, EVER been in the paper before.

It turned out that the woman on allotment number seven used to be a midwife. So Grandad had borrowed an old stethoscope from her. And, every morning, he would listen in on the pumpkin. Not that it had a heartbeat, but Grandad said that he could hear the juices and the waters flowing in it. Once they stopped, the pumpkin would be ready to pick, he'd told Marty. Well, when he said 'pick', he meant it would be time to borrow the Japanese ceremonial sword hanging from the wall of the Crown and Anchor and hack through the thick vine that held it on to the plant.

After the picture in the paper, LOADS more people came to look at the pumpkin. It became almost like a shrine, somewhere people wanted to be. Gracie and Grandad had been to the pound shop to get some paper cups and were selling tea and coffee for fifty pence a go too. The piece in the paper had done its job beautifully and the more people told it their dreams and wishes, the more people came, and the more it grew. It was as if, for once in their lives, they could speak to something that was listening.

'You all right, Marty?'

Marty couldn't actually believe his eyes. He had known one or two of the people who had come to see the pumpkin, but it was truly strange to see Mr Garraway there.

'I'm OK, thanks.'

'Good, aye,' Mr Garraway replied looking rather embarrassed. 'Where do I put my fifty pence?'

Marty nodded to the bucket, and he smiled as Mr Garraway circled the pumpkin and whispered something under his breath.

The night before, as he lay in the shed listening to Grandad snore, Marty had thought about how the pumpkin drew people in. It was as if they were entranced by nature. That they couldn't quite believe that something so wonderful and massive and magical could be real. He couldn't believe it himself sometimes. He'd wake, peer out of the door of the shed, and there it would be. Silver and magnificent under the moon. Their wondrous ship, waiting to be pushed into the water on her maiden voyage. Children would laugh when they saw it; grown men would go speechless. It was something extraordinary in the midst of the ordinariness of their lives. Marty had even asked Grandad whether it might get too big with wishes and explode, but Grandad had shaken his head sagely and assured Marty that no one and nothing could ever be *too* full of dreams.

Today Grandad was listening intently to the pumpkin's insides. He shouted across at Gracie and Marty.

'It's almost time, you know. It's almost time . . .'

Gracie had brought the life jackets to the shed. The outboard motor and the expanding foam to seal it to the side of the pumpkin was there as well. Grandad had borrowed a Japanese ceremonial sword from the wall of the public house downstairs from his bedsit, so they had the cutting sorted. All the wish money and the tea-and-coffee kitty had paid for supplies to take with them. It was just a matter of waiting.

Marty was the only one who hadn't fulfilled his promise of getting the rope and the material for the sail. He had kept meaning to go. He knew where they were in the garden. He knew where everything was – he didn't even have to go into the house – but he just kept putting it off. It was seeing his mum that would be too painful, and, let's face it, she was always going to be there.

Grandad let Marty listen to the pumpkin for a moment. He pressed the earbuds into his ears and placed the stethoscope on the pumpkin's side. *Whoosh, whoosh, whoosh!*

'It's alive!'

Grandad laughed.

'Of course it is!'

Gracie came near, and Marty reached out and tapped out the pumpkin's rhythm on to her back so she could feel it too. Gracie smiled.

That evening, Grandad and Marty sat around the fire watching Gracie dance. Her audition was in a few days, just before they had to set sail. She had become a bit quieter recently and Marty could tell she was thinking about it a lot.

'I spoke to your mum, Marty . . .' said Grandad.

Marty's eyes flicked to his face. 'Why?'

'Check if she was all right . . .'

Marty didn't want to ask if she was, even though he really wanted to know.

'I know maybe you think I'm hard on your mother . . .'

Marty kept watching the flames.

'I have tried, over the years. When you were small . . . I . . . I thought maybe it was my fault somehow. That I made her like that. That I grew her wrong.'

Marty thought about this and, for the first time ever, he saw something approaching uncertainty in Grandad's eyes.

'No,' said Marty. 'It's an illness . . . That's what the doctors say . . .' Marty had always clung to that thought. He shrugged. 'I dunno, Grandad, sometimes my brain aches just thinking about it.'

'But I know she's proud of you, boy . . .'

Marty bit his lip.

'All grown up! Starting your journey.'

Marty smiled.

'And look at me! An old man . . .'

'You're not old,' Marty said, before looking up at Grandad earnestly. 'You're absolutely ancient . . .'

Grandad laughed his belly laugh and looked up into the sky for a moment.

'You know . . .' He hesitated. 'I used to wonder what it would be like to be old . . .'

Marty watched his face, the shadows flickering across it in the darkness.

'What does it feel like?'

Grandad shrugged.

'I don't know. I feel exactly like I did back when I was young, except I have to get up three times every night to pee.'

Marty laughed.

'Right, then.' Grandad stood up. 'I'm going to get some beauty sleep.'

Grandad was going back to the bedsit tonight. Gracie was staying with Marty in the shed. She'd told her dad she was having a sleepover with a friend, which was technically true. Marty watched Grandad get up creakily and brush off his trousers before winding his way along the path towards the bedsit.

Marty watched Gracie dance until she had finished practising and he promised himself that however old he got, he wouldn't let himself know what it felt like either.

CHAPTER TWENTY-THREE

There was no point whispering to Gracie because she took her sound processor off at night, so he gave her a nudge. When she groaned as she came to, Marty raised a finger to his lips to indicate for her to stay quiet. All he could see in the moonlight were her wide-open eyes. He gestured outside with the other hand and mouthed . . .

'There's someone here!'

He listened. Got up quietly. Gestured for Gracie to do the same. They normally slept in their clothes here anyway as it was cold at night. They edged out and Marty heard voices at the other side of the allotment. Gracie pulled up her sleeve to reveal her watch; it was three o'clock in the morning.

Marty pulled her behind the shed. It was the new-trainer kids; he was sure it was. The voices and laughter got nearer and nearer, bits of conversation being carried on the breeze . . .

'Little show-off . . .'

'Gets his ugly face in the paper and thinks he's it.'

Yes, it was definitely them. Marty's heart started racing. They'd known this was a possibility, but two minutes ago he'd been fast asleep, and being woken by voices in the middle of the night made you feel dizzy. Like it wasn't really happening.

He heard the allotment gate creak. They were ready for this. They had made their preparations. But now the time was here Marty had got literal and figurative cold feet. Gracie nudged him and mouthed, *'What's going on?'*

'They're coming up the path . . .' Marty mouthed back.

It was dark and it was making it difficult for Gracie to lip-read.

They'd laid a system of pulleys and traps. They knew what to do – it was a well-oiled and meticulously drilled operation. Marty shuffled over to one side of the shed and leaned down to pick up a rope laid on the floor. Gracie kept watch the other side. Then, when the boys were halfway up the path, she signalled thumbs-up. Marty then yanked the rope, which pulled on a pulley and raised a wire, thin and invisible, as taut as a guitar string, across the path.

There was a second and a half of silence, before the first one fell, *CRUMP!* Then, another one fell over the first one, '*WAAAAA!*' Then another one, *SPLAT*.

Marty peeped round the side of the shed to see a lump of flailing and kicking arms and legs wriggling on the path. He tried not to giggle.

'Get off me! Get off me!'

'What are you doing? Watch where you're going, you idiot!'

'It wasn't me! It was him!'

Marty gave Gracie the thumbs-up. There were three of them, from what Marty could count in the dim light. He watched as they got up, untangled themselves and started shoving each other as each one tried to blame the other.

'Let's do this!' said Gerry eventually. 'We came here to give that pumpkin a kicking, and that's what we're going to do . . . We'll show them and that stupid wishing pumpkin . . .'

Marty's eyes narrowed. They were truly horrible. Absolutely horrible. He watched as they walked nearer the shed. Although they were all mouth, Marty was convinced that they looked a bit uncertain. It was almost as if they were afraid of being out in the dark. He smiled. This was going to be so much fun. Marty had a secret weapon stashed behind the shed. It was one of the lady at allotment seven's wind chimes. He picked it up and blew on it. An eerie sound reverberated around the allotment. Marty listened as the boys stopped in their tracks.

'What was that?'

They listened for a moment.

'It was nothing.'

Marty blew again so the chimes shivered in the night.

'There it was again!'

'It's a ghost!'

'There's no such thing!'

'I heard it!'

'Are you stupid or what? I said there's no such thing as ghosts!'

'That wasn't a normal sound . . .'

Marty stifled a giggle. They were truly on edge now,

but for step three of the plan he and Gracie needed them to get closer to the pumpkin. Marty put the windchimes down and let them walk closer. As they did so, his throat tightened. He knew what they wanted to do to it, but in order to get this just right he had to let them get close. Just close enough . . .

'Cor,' said one, his dull voice bouncing off the pumpkin, 'look at the size of it!'

It does seem to strike awe in people, even stupid ones, thought Marty.

Gracie kicked him and he gestured upward and mouthed . . . '*After three.*'

He watched as they inched closer . . . closer . . . their white trainers shining in the moonlight.

'This is gonna be ace!' said Gerry, giggling stupidly. 'Ready?' he asked.

Marty nodded at Gracie and stuck up his fingers . . . one, two and three.

Gracie yanked down on the chain hanging from the top of the shed, and the bucket of fish guts flew out of the nearby tree and upended itself all over the three boys.

'Jesus!' shrieked one.

'What happened?'

Gerry had had his mouth open in shock and had got a mouthful of fish guts. He was dabbing at his tongue with fishy hands, which made everything worse.

'Oh my GOD! WHAT IS THAT?'

'It stinks!'

'Let's get out of here . . . !'

'NOW!'

Marty pulled another chain and – *WHOOSH* – another bucket flew through the night and dumped a load of slimy seaweed tea all over them.

'This place is haunted!' screamed one as he slipped on to his bum on the ground.

They wriggled and writhed and couldn't for the life of them stand up. Then, for good measure, Gracie let rip with a bucket of nettle stink tonic.

'*WAAAAAAAAAAAAA!*' They didn't know which way was up by now.

Marty was giggling and so was Gracie, both of them holding on to the sides of the shed for dear life.

The white-trainer boys looked like swamp monsters: green and black with arms and legs flailing everywhere, making the most disturbing sounds anyone had ever heard. When they eventually got to their feet, they scrabbled and grappled with each other as they made for the gate.

Marty knew that this final touch was a bit show-offy. It wasn't necessary, really, but he thought it might add to the artistic sense of this occasion. There was only one rope left, and it was attached to a crate by the gate. In it were twenty of the lady from number seven's pigeons. They were lovely birds, but were used to racing. One tug on the rope and they'd burst from the cage in an explosion of feathers and cooing. Marty knew that when he tugged, the little door would open and – *WHOOSH* – off they would go.

He watched as the boys struggled nearer the gate before beaming at Gracie . . .

CHAPTER TWENTY-FOUR

'Hey, Grandad, is Marty here?'

Grandad straightened his back.

'He's gone to get some supplies . . .' He winked at Gracie. She was leaning on the old rickety fence. Grandad could see there was a stillness about her that wasn't usually there.

'Don't suppose you fancy making me a cup of tea, do you?' he chanced, sensing that sitting quietly a while might help her.

Gracie smiled warmly.

'Go on, then . . .' she replied.

Grandad watched as she put the kettle on and set about fishing out some very dodgy-looking teabags from a damp cardboard box.

'So, you all ready for the dance competition tomorrow, then? I can't believe it's come round so fast!' Grandad was wiping his hands on a cloth so dirty that it wouldn't make much difference.

'Think so . . .'

Grandad looked at her as she handed him his mug. She took her own and they went to sit outside the shed.

'I'm catching the train first thing in the morning . . .'

'Isn't your dad taking you?'

Gracie shrugged. 'I'll be back by tomorrow night so I can get to bed early before we sail.'

'You don't seem too excited?' Grandad ventured. 'About the audition, I mean.'

Gracie glanced away, her mug steaming into the air.

'I am. It's just . . . Oh, I don't know.'

She looked as if she wanted to say something else, so Grandad said nothing and gave her a little time.

'We get on. Dad and me. Not like you and Marty, though.'

Grandad listened.

'Mum and him split up and, since then, he's been like a headless chicken. Trying to set up a new business.

Trying to do stuff all the time. Worrying about the future . . .'

Grandad considered this.

'I can't speak for all men, but, sometimes, doing stuff is the only way they can show they care.'

Gracie looked down at her tea.

'I know.'

Grandad waited a moment.

'Look, Gracie, I made a lot of mistakes with my little girl. I loved her . . . I love her with all my heart, but every time I opened my mouth I'd say something wrong. So I stopped. I stopped talking. We both stopped talking.'

Grandad stopped a moment. He was rarely this serious.

'It's been one of my biggest regrets.'

Grandad heard voices in the distance. The first of the day's visitors to the pumpkin.

'She was and is my little girl. Always has been. Always will be. And that's a special thing.'

Gracie looked thoughtful.

'You're going to be brilliant tomorrow; you know that . . .'

Gracie seemed a little unsure.

'And, anyway, if you start to tense up, just think about what you and Marty did to those bullies.'

Gracie's face softened into a smile. 'Right, tell Marty I'll see him the day after tomorrow. I'd better go and pack . . .' She was about to get up when her face became serious. 'I can't believe it's time . . . the audition and our trip . . .'

Grandad listened.

Gracie sighed. 'It's a lot, isn't it?'

Grandad smiled. 'It's good to be nervous.' He winked. 'It's a sign that you care. Just take those nerves and use them as energy to blow their socks off.'

Gracie's face relaxed as they both got to their feet.

'Now, you go get 'em and come back here for the adventure of your life!'

Gracie squished him into a quick hug before letting go. 'Thanks,' she said.

Grandad nodded. 'You're more than welcome, my lovely.'

He watched her go before turning to watch the crowds start to file solemnly past the pumpkin.

*

Marty had put off going home to collect the old rope and sailcloth as long as he could, but they needed them now and it was impossible to avoid it any longer. He'd actually sat on the swing in the empty park behind the estate for a while to work himself up to it, and it was getting late in the afternoon by the time he actually started walking towards his mum's house.

It was weird. Going back. It had only been a couple of months, but it felt like forever. He'd managed not to try to imagine Mum alone in the house, sitting in that stupid chair. Whenever he felt his mind starting to slip that way, he'd yank it back. He knew she had to face this alone, and that he had to give her space to do that, while he, well, while he got on with it.

He turned the corner by the cycle path and saw the estate from a distance. He didn't actually have a plan. He didn't think he'd stay and talk, but, then again, he didn't really know how he'd feel until he saw her.

He stepped into the garden. The mess was the same. He tried to harden his heart again. Swallow down any feeling so he wouldn't be caught unaware. The back door was open. He knew where the rope was. It was curled up inside an old washing machine in the garden. He approached the washing machine, pressed its metal button and watched as the door flew open. Inside, sure enough, was the rope.

The sailcloth was outside by the window of the back room, rolled up under an old zinc sheet. He stumbled his way towards the window. Tried not to make too much noise. It was weird. He almost felt like a robber or a thief. He shifted up the metal sheet and dragged the sailcloth out. Then he heard voices. He stood stock still for a moment. He was sure there were two. A man's voice as well as his mum's. He stuffed the sailcloth under his armpit and smudged his nose closer to the window.

Inside was his mum, sitting in her chair. She looked thinner somehow. And opposite her where Marty used to sit on a pile of newspapers was a man. He studied him. It wasn't his dad. It was someone else and, more than that, they were laughing together. Marty listened. He hadn't heard her laugh like that in years. They were drinking tea. The man was sitting, relaxed and happy; they obviously knew each other pretty well. They looked like friends . . .

He looked back at his mum, and thought that she looked different. It wasn't just that her hair was clean and tied back or that she was laughing; there was a lightness about her. Marty pulled back, his heart sinking. He didn't want to admit it to himself, but he'd thought that she might just be a *little* heartbroken that he wasn't there any more. He listened to them giggle once more, before making his way back across the garden.

He walked back to the allotment, the rope round his shoulder and the sailcloth under his arm. By the time he arrived, it was getting dark. Grandad had brought some food from the bedsit and set up a supper by the fire. He noticed that a silence was hanging around Marty like a mist.

'You OK?' Grandad asked.

Marty shrugged, unable to shift the sound of his mum's giggling from his head.

'I'm fine,' he said, but Grandad looked unconvinced.

After supper, they sat in silence, Grandad hoicked a pair of old reading glasses on to his nose and handed Marty some thread. Marty had to thread the needle as that was too much for Grandad's eyes. He then sat on

the floor under the thick cloth, pushing the needle back through the sail towards Grandad. Marty watched the needle appear and disappear and thought about what was about to happen.

CHAPTER TWENTY-FIVE

'Marty! . . . Come on, boy . . . Wake up!'

Marty groaned, rubbed his eyes and squinted. Grandad was crouched down beside him, shaking him, the stethoscope round his neck.

'There's no sound. The pumpkin. It's ready! It's absolutely chocka! Full to the brim with wishes.'

'What?'

'It's time to open up that beauty!'

You could almost feel the excitement radiating off Grandad. Marty shuffled to sit upright, his hair doing inexplicable things.

'Well.' Grandad looked at him irritably. 'Come on, then! Don't you know how much work we've got to do?'

Even at 8 a.m., a crowd had already started gathering

as Marty drank his tea and finger-brushed his teeth. There were people everywhere – not just Sadiq and John Trinidad and Colin. Everyone knew the pumpkin was almost fully grown and there were wild rumours circulating about what would happen next. Grandad was in his element.

A murmur went around. A buzz as Grandad leaned an old ladder up against the side of the pumpkin. People took pictures on their phones. Grandad and Marty grabbed the ceremonial sword from the pub between them and, on three, they hacked through the stem.

A loud cheer went up.

The pumpkin, of course, didn't move. It wasn't about to bounce away, weighing about three tonnes, as it did. What they needed to do now was remove the stalk end, just a rounded opening, exactly like a Halloween pumpkin, and scoop out the insides. However, this was on a completely different scale.

The pumpkin's skin was so thick that it seemed actually impenetrable, and this was why Grandad had borrowed Colin's chainsaw. Grandad threw down a rope and Colin tied the chainsaw to it so it could be hoicked up, as climbing up a ladder with a chainsaw is probably not a great idea. Grandad pulled it up the bulging side of the pumpkin and Marty watched as Grandad filled the chainsaw with petrol from a canister and fired it up. It mewed and roared in the morning sunshine. Another round of clapping erupted.

The first cut was amazing, and Marty wished that Gracie had been there to see it. It was as if the pumpkin absorbed the noise from the chainsaw and reverberated it around its whole massive body. It transferred into a wibble of excitement in everyone's stomachs. Grandad paused for a moment and threw off his trilby, then he turned up his shirt sleeves. He cut and cut, firmly but gently, like a surgeon, wanting to turn this pumpkin into something wondrous rather than hurt it or damage it. Then, eventually, he switched the chainsaw off.

'Chuck us up the shovel, Colin!' Grandad cried.

Colin did as he was told. Then Grandad slid the spade into the cut he'd made and jammed his foot down hard to lift the lid of the pumpkin. He was sweating already. It shifted, then croaked.

'Come on, Grandad!' said Marty.

'Lord, it's heavy!' Grandad panted.

Marty went round beside him and added his weight to the shovel and – *CRRRRRREAK* – it came away, a giant circle of pumpkin the size of a round table. Then several pairs of hands appeared from below, ready to slide it safely on to the raised bed on the other side.

Another cheer.

Grandad wiped his brow and he and Marty looked inside the beast for the first time. Marty gasped. It was wondrous. Absolutely full to the brim with seeds. Giant pumpkin seeds, the size of mangoes, stringy membranes and bright orange flesh. It cast a golden glow up on to their faces. Marty could see the wonder on his grandad's face and, in that moment, he loved him for it. Grandad looked up at him . . .

'Let's get these seeds out . . .'

Grandad asked everyone to leave while they set about emptying the pumpkin, but he invited them to come back the following morning and promised them a magnificent sight. Some of them grumbled, but most were cheery, telling them to call if they needed any help.

When the crowd had gone, and after Grandad and

Marty had had a cup of tea, they started the job in earnest. Taking a shovel each, they stood on top of the pumpkin, digging out the seeds and dropping them by the kilo into the plastic buckets. When they ran out of those, they filled the wheelbarrow and then the water butts and then anything and everything else they could find. They worked until the sun was high in the sky before the lady from allotment seven brought them some lunch. After that, they started again. It was wondrous, that something this big could produce what seemed like an infinite number of new seeds. New beginnings. Grandad wanted them to be stored carefully so they could be kept.

By early evening, they had managed to scrape all the seeds out, and you couldn't even see Marty and Grandad working as they were in the depths of the pumpkin. As they got deeper and deeper, their voices boomed inside the pumpkin and Grandad's laughter was amplified all around Marty. Later on, they cut a circle out of the side of the pumpkin where Grandad had calculated the waterline would be. They had estimated the mass and volume of the pumpkin, and Grandad had worked out a likely position for it. Then, they squeezed in the outboard engine and sealed the gaps around it with the expanding foam, which seemed to work a treat. Later in the evening, Sadiq brought over some stew – it was delicious – and he helped them clear up a bit so the place was presentable for the morning.

The last jobs were to place two planks in the pumpkin across the inside so they'd have somewhere to sit, and to erect the sail so they'd have wind power even if the engine failed. They set up the mast between the horizontal planks and hauled the sail up it so it sat in a perfect triangle. Grandad was good at knots, so he did those, and by the time the sun had started to set it was ready.

Marty and Grandad sat down, exhausted. Their arms ached. Their backs ached too, but neither of them had ever felt so happy. The pumpkin was a beauty, an absolute stunner. A dream realized. Marty just looked at her, her majestic sail flapping gently in the moonlight.

'Tomorrow morning, we sail,' murmured Grandad quietly.

Marty looked at him and, for the first time, saw a tired look in his eyes.

'It's going to be great!' Grandad said. 'We'll show them!'

Marty glanced towards Gracie's house.

Grandad followed his gaze. 'I thought Gracie was supposed to be back tonight?' he asked, scratching his head.

Marty nodded. 'She was.'

Grandad frowned.

'Something must've come up.' Marty shrugged. 'I'm sure she'll be here by morning.'

Marty had soon fallen into a deep sleep, but the cold woke him up. He got up, rummaged around in the shed for Gracie's sleeping bag and draped it over himself to keep warm, before realizing that Grandad wasn't there.

'Grandad?' he asked the darkness. No reply. Marty frowned and lay back down again. He was probably outside making some last-minute preparations. Marty closed his eyes. Tomorrow was going to be a very big day.

Grandad looked up at the house and pulled off his hat. There was a light on inside. He cleared his throat and knocked gingerly at the door. He heard footsteps on the tiles inside.

Gracie's dad opened the door and looked out into

the gloom. He was clearly not happy to find Grandad standing there wearing the dirty, smelly jacket he always wore on the allotment.

'You! What on earth do you want?' he asked irritably.

'You're Gracie's dad, aren't you?' said Grandad. 'I think you and me should have a little talk.'

CHAPTER TWENTY-SIX

The auditions had overrun. They had had so many people trying out that the queue had snaked all along the corridor and outside the building and down the street. Gracie actually couldn't believe it. She'd had to queue outside for almost the whole day and then, when she was just about at the front, they had closed the door and told everyone to come back in the morning.

Gracie had tried to protest, but they wouldn't listen. Marty and Grandad would be opening the pumpkin today and she was supposed to be making her way home ready to sail in the morning. She'd tried to leave a message for them, but since Grandad only had a phone in his flat and they'd been staying at the allotment, she hadn't had much hope of them getting it. The organizers of the competition had offered a bed for the night to anyone who had travelled far, and Gracie had accepted, saying that her dad was with her.

After she'd reached the cheap hotel, she'd texted her dad, saying that she was staying at Poppy's house for another night and had crossed her fingers that he wouldn't ring and check. Then she'd lain on the bed feeling as if her heart were being torn in two. She really, really wanted to do the competition. After all, she'd put so much work into it, but she also really, really wanted to sail with Marty and Grandad.

She hardly slept a wink.

In the morning, she'd got up and come straight back to the audition venue, thinking if she arrived extra early she might be able to compete and still make it home in time. She had stood, agitatedly, in line with the other girls, who had been chatting to each other happily. They obviously knew each other from their dance classes. Their hair was tied in tight buns and they had regulation clothes on. Gracie had run her fingers through her hair: she hadn't tied it back, and her clothes were, well, not regulation.

At last it was Gracie's turn. She stood in the middle of the dance studio. The judges were sitting in a line. Four of them looking at her. One of them cleared her throat.

'So, which dance will you be performing?'

Gracie looked at her lips.

'Well,' she said, looking sideways and then to the floor. 'It's a dance I made up . . .'

One of the other judges sat back, a bored look on his face.

'Oh really?'

Gracie nodded.

'And how long have you been dancing?' another woman asked.

Gracie could feel herself getting hot. Too hot.

'Er, I don't know. About as long as I've been breathing, I suppose.'

'I see,' she said tartly.

Gracie watched as they looked at her with bemusement.

'And . . .' said the last woman. 'Which grade are you? Which disciplines do you study? Ballet? Modern? Tap?'

Gracie had dreaded this question. She looked squarely at them. Tried to stand tall.

'None – I mean, I haven't had any training.'

Even from this distance, Gracie could see she'd raised an eyebrow.

'None at all?' The lady's expression was icy.

Gracie could sense the other girls who were left in the corridor outside the door obviously listening in. She wanted to run. She wanted to hide. She could feel her chest burning up.

'And what's the inspiration for your piece?'

Gracie had thought about the story. She'd thought about what she should say, but she couldn't explain it as well with words as she could with her body. She shrugged.

'I don't know. I guess it's about sounds . . .'

There was another pause before the first judge spoke at last.

'OK, then,' she said. 'Well, let's see what you can do, shall we?'

Gracie nodded, glad of the chance to just stop talking.

'I'll need the music loud,' she said, and looked at the panel once again.

They smiled. Looked at her implant. 'Of course,' one replied.

Gracie ran to the side of the room and slipped off her shoes. Then she switched off her sound processor and took a deep breath. She ran back to the middle of the room. They all watched as she centred herself. The music grew and started filling the room. She closed her eyes, and raised herself up on to her toes. She waited . . . waited . . . waited for the waves of music to move her . . . she hung on . . . in suspended animation, like a wave reaching its peak before breaking into white water. She hung in the air . . . a little longer and a little longer . . . and then she danced . . .

'I've done it all wrong, haven't I?'

Gracie almost jumped out of her skin. Her heart was still thumping after the audition and her face felt flushed. She'd just switched her sound processor back on and was pulling on her shoes in the cloakroom when her dad spoke. 'I'm sorry, Gracie.'

Gracie couldn't actually believe her eyes.

'Er, shouldn't you be at work?'

'Probably.'

'Who . . . ? What . . . ? Who told you, anyway?'

Gracie's dad smiled.

'It doesn't matter. I drove up here last night. I was worried sick . . .'

Gracie didn't know what to say. She was half bracing

herself for the comeuppance that was bound to be coming her way

'Am I in trouble?'

He shook his head. 'No.'

'What? Like, really?'

'I saw you dance, Gracie.'

Gracie felt her heart lurch once again.

'It was beautiful and you're right . . .'

'About what?' asked Gracie.

'Since your mum left . . . I've been trying to cope. To fix things. To keep busy and . . .'

'Do something?' Gracie offered.

Her dad nodded.

'I know,' Gracie said.

He looked tired. Worn out.

'I don't actually need you to *do* anything, Dad . . . I just . . .' Gracie shrugged, felt the tears tighten her throat.

Her dad got up. Came towards her and hugged her.

'I want you to know that I never doubted you. I knew you were brilliant. I knew you could do anything. It was just I forgot that maybe you have your own ideas . . . It's just . . . the world can be a cruel place.'

Gracie sniffed. Despite herself, the tears were warming her face now. She looked up at him.

'It can also be a wonderful place . . .'

Her dad looked down at her.

'It is . . . and I think I lost sight of that for a little while there . . .'

He kissed her head and they stood for a long time.

'You stink . . .' he said after a while. 'You're all sweaty.'

Gracie laughed, stepped back. Rubbed her face with her hands. They smiled at each other.

'I know.'

'So?' he asked. 'What do you want to do now?'

'Well . . .' Gracie said, looking at her watch. 'I'm glad you asked me that . . .'

CHAPTER TWENTY-SEVEN

'GOOD MORNING, SUNSHINE! TAKE A PEE BEHIND THE RHUBARB! CHANGE YOUR UNDERPANTS! HAVE SOME BREAKFAST! TODAY WE SAILLLLLLLLL!'

Grandad was bouncing. Marty squinted.

'What time is it?'

Grandad looked at his watch.

'Four in the morning . . . Come on! Up and at 'em!'

Marty saw that Grandad had been revived, then.

Colin, Sadiq and the lady from allotment seven were already there. Grandad had scrambled a load of eggs in a frying pan on the fire and everyone was chomping down. At half past five the skinny journalist from the paper turned up, his eye twitching, ready to take some pictures along with what seemed like half the city. One person had messaged their friends, and they had messaged their friends, until the crowd became enormous! Everyone stood gasping and wondering, goggling and guessing.

As the sun began to climb in the sky, it showed off the pumpkin boat in all her glory. She was bright and enormous. Breathtaking. The skinny man scratched his head before Grandad leaned a ladder on the side of the pumpkin and climbed up into it. Then he clapped so that everyone would listen.

'We had a seed of an idea, a little, tiny seed. Then we planted it and watched it grow! I present to you HMS *Sailing Seed*!'

Everyone gasped.

'We're going to sail across the Channel in this here boat today.'

People were absolutely gobsmacked. The skinny man started to scribble down his notes. This was a scoop. The scoop of all scoops. If he could get some pictures to the newsroom this morning, he might even make the nine o'clock headlines. All the television services would be after the story too, and he was here. *CLICK. CLICK. CLICK.* He took hundreds of pictures.

'This adventure is for all of us!' said Grandad. 'Us dreamers! Us people they say are mad and bonkers! This is our way of saying, "We matter too." This is our way of saying, "Don't ever let go of your dreams."'

People were going crazy. Phones were clicking. Children were cheering. Marty watched, spellbound.

'Now, we need help. We need to get this pumpkin on to the back of that milk float so we can take it down to that harbour.'

Colin had backed the milk float on to next door's allotment. They could then drive it down the road and join the motorway to the coast. Marty had filled the pumpkin with bottles of water and packets of food and the fireworks that had been left over after last year's bonfire night at the pub.

They were all there, all the familiar faces. Marty even recognized some from school. Mr Garraway gave him the thumbs-up. The only face he couldn't find was Gracie's. He frowned, but was shouted at for dithering.

'Heave ho! Heave ho!'

Grandads and grandmas, kids and brothers and sisters and mums and dads helped. Aunties and uncles and friends and passers-by rocked and rolled the pumpkin. They pressed their hands on to it, pushed it and pulled it, until its fat belly lolled off the raised bed and sat slung between the planks and the back of the milk float.

'Heave ho! Heave ho!'

They started again. Everyone straining and sweating. Heaving and ho-ing. The suspension on the milk float sank about thirty centimetres when the weight started to shift on to the back. For a moment there, Marty thought the pumpkin might flip that little float upside down

like a tiddlywink. They shifted and shunted, they pulled and pushed until, in the end, the pumpkin sat, fat and squat, on the back. A loud cheer went up as everyone celebrated. Several of the tallest people then helped tie the pumpkin in place.

'Right, come on, Marty – we'll sit up front with Colin,' said Grandad.

They had to leave pronto as the tide was currently in. If they waited any longer, they'd miss their window of opportunity.

Marty was looking around frantically. Grandad read his mind.

'Something must've come up with Gracie. Come on . . .'

Marty grabbed his coat and jumped into the passenger seat of the milk float as the engine whined into life. It sounded like a lawnmower engine, straining and heaving against the enormous weight in the back.

Colin tapped the dashboard – 'Come on, Bessy!' – and then they were off.

I suppose it's not every day that you see a giant pumpkin boat driving down the motorway on the back of a milk float, not least because it's probably highly illegal. But this wasn't just any day. Marty thought they might get a bit of attention, but he certainly wasn't expecting this.

There was a convoy of cars behind them. Cars of well-wishers and newspaper reporters and people curious about what was going on. It really was quite the circus. And it was a fairly long drive – long enough for Marty to start getting nervous. What if they'd calculated everything wrong? What if they placed HMS *Sailing Seed* in the water and she just sank to the bottom with a great big bubble of a burp? Marty came out in a cold sweat. What if they did actually sink in the middle of the sea? He could swim, sure, but not for nearly a hundred miles . . .

Grandad obviously sensed his quietness. 'Marty, don't worry . . .'

'I'm not worrying . . .' he lied.

'Yes you are . . .'

The milk float engine had started to smoke by now; it was billowing into the cab, making Marty and Grandad and Colin cough.

'You're doing this for all of us,' said Colin.

Marty hadn't really spent much time up close with

him before. He was huge, of course, Marty had noticed that, but there was a real softness in his eyes.

'All those things I used to think up . . .' Colin said with a sad little smile. 'Never came to anything . . . I used to want to be a nurse.'

Marty was surprised by that.

'Everyone laughed, said I couldn't do it. So I did the really stupid thing and listened to them.'

Grandad shook his head.

'And the funny thing is I don't even like flippin' milk . . .' He now stuck his chin out. 'I'm going to get you to that harbour if it's the last thing I do . . .'

The harbour was already jam packed with cars. They'd overtaken the milk float on the motorway and had tried to get themselves in the best position for taking pictures. Colin backed the milk float down on to the slipway. The sea looked calm and perfect. It couldn't have been better. Grandad and Marty jumped out.

'How are we going to do this?' asked Marty.

Grandad hadn't actually worked this one out. There was a step, he noticed. If they pushed the pumpkin off, then they'd run the risk of smashing it. It would be too heavy, even for a whole crowd to lift. Grandad looked distressed.

'We're almost there! We're almost there!' Colin puffed out his chest. 'Get in it,' he said.

'What?' asked Grandad.

'Get in it, you and Marty.'

'What are you going to do?'

'I'll back her up to the edge of the water, jump out and let her sink.'

'The milk float? You sure?'

Colin looked like he'd never been surer of anything in his whole life.

'I'm not going to need it any more. I'm going back to college.'

Grandad smiled. 'Genius . . .' Then he placed a hand on Marty's shoulder. 'Come on, boy. It's time.'

Marty and Grandad jumped into the pumpkin. Grandad had his hand on the engine and Marty raised the sail. There was a slight breeze. The crowd on the quayside were shouting. There was even a helicopter overhead.

'Three! TWO! ONEEEEE!'

The crowd quietened down and watched with bated breath as Colin the milkman revved the engine and started reversing. They gasped as the milk float started picking up speed as it backed up towards the sea. Then they let out a huge cheer when, at the water's edge, Colin jumped out with a massive grin on his face.

'Hold on, Marty!' cried Grandad.

And, smooth as you like, the van rolled into the water and sank away into the depths, leaving Grandad and Marty bobbing about on the surface. Marty clung on to the sides of the pumpkin for dear life and Grandad laughed until he ached. They couldn't actually hear anything any more as the crowd on the quayside had gone quite hysterical with cheering.

'This is the best day of my life!' cried Grandad. Then he started up the engine.

The pumpkin bobbed and tilted, wobbled and jerked, until eventually the motor built up a nice rhythm and, suddenly, they were moving! They were going out to sea.

Grandad shook the sail out, caught the direction of the wind and off they went. It was weird: although they couldn't hear a thing by the harbour, once they were only a few hundred metres out to sea, it got drastically quieter. Like they were bobbing into the unknown.

But there was one voice – one voice that kept shouting.

'Wait! WAIT!'

Marty was sure it was coming from above. He looked up and saw the helicopter hovering above them. It was blue with a red stripe. A coastguard helicopter, in fact. Marty squinted his eyes; it was making the water choppy for the pumpkin.

'What's it doing?' asked Grandad.

'There's someone dangling from a rope!'

Sure enough, the helicopter was dangling a figure in a life jacket towards the pumpkin.

'It's Gracie!' Marty beamed.

And it was!

Grandad steered the boat so she could fall into the pumpkin unhurt. She landed with a thud and an 'I'm all right'.

Marty hugged her.

'What on earth . . . ?'

Gracie righted herself and puffed out her cheeks.

'Don't even ask!'

CHAPTER TWENTY-EIGHT

O nce the land had slipped out of view, the sea became a bit quieter. The waves would flop a little on the side of the pumpkin, but other than that, and the flight of a few birds, it was quiet. Heavenly. Marty's heart had settled into its normal rhythm, but even though he knew it was real, he could hardly believe it! They were sailing. Actually sailing. Grandad was checking his compass and his map every now and again, and they spent the first few hours in silent awe as if they didn't actually have the words to express how they were feeling.

At lunchtime, Grandad set a course with the engine and they all had a picnic in the pumpkin in the middle of the sea.

'You get in, then?' Marty asked Gracie at last, as if

chatting to a friend while bobbling about in the middle of the sea in a pumpkin was entirely normal.

Gracie shrugged her shoulders as she shared out the sandwiches.

'You have to wait for them to call you . . . or not . . .'

'So, what was with the coastguard helicopter?'

Gracie grinned.

'The auditions overran; I thought I'd never get here. Anyway, turns out someone had told my dad where I was . . .'

At this, Grandad started to fake whistle and look away.

'Who told your . . . ?' Marty clicked. 'Grandad! How could you?'

'It's all right! It's all right!' Gracie laughed. 'Anyway, he saw me dance, we had a good talk and then . . . You remember me saying that Dad used to do a bit of sailing? Turns out he knew the coastguard and one of them actually owed him a favour . . . I couldn't actually believe he was doing it, but next thing I knew – this helicopter turned up . . .'

Marty had never seen Gracie laugh when she talked about her father before.

'And, ta-da. Here I am! After seeing how I managed at the audition, I think Dad has realized that, you know, I can look after myself.'

Marty smiled at her. 'That's good,' he said.

'He told me to tell you thanks, Grandad.' Gracie grinned.

Grandad grinned back. 'It's quite all right, my dear.'

'So, what are we doing when we get to Paris?' she said, changing the subject.

'Well,' said Grandad, sitting down at last and helping himself to a cheese and pickle. 'I've worked it all out.' He took a notepad out of the top pocket of his waistcoat. 'We want to make the most of our trip, so I made us a schedule. We park up the pumpkin, quick walk into the city. Swift recce around the Louvre, lunch in Jardin des Tuileries and a quick trip up the Eiffel Tower to see the Paris lights in the evening. Back to the pumpkin to sleep and start home in the morning. What do you say?'

'Sounds like a plan. The Eiffel Tower. What do you think, Marty?' said Gracie, studying his face.

'Sounds perfect,' he replied, trying hard not to let his mind drift in the direction of his father, or to wonder how many other seemingly impossible things might turn out to be possible during this adventure, after all.

'This is great, though, don't you think?' Gracie smiled.

Marty grinned. It was. It absolutely was.

After lunchtime, Grandad calculated that they must be about halfway to Le Havre. He had worked out that they could cover twenty-five miles an hour. So, the 127 between Southampton and Le Havre could technically be covered in around five hours.

Every now and again, the silence would be broken by a boat sailing nearby or a ferry in the distance. Marty looked into the water and watched as jellyfish bobbed up and down, spotting the sea with their blobbiness, and Gracie almost jumped out of her seat when she saw a pod of dolphins surface nearby.

'Ha ha!' shouted Grandad.

Grandad was in charge of the engine, and with topping it up with petrol from the canisters in the bottom of the boat. Marty was in charge of the sail, and he would sit with the old compass Grandad had given him balancing on his knees, and look up at the sail every now and again. He could feel the wind in it. Feel it catch the sail and hurry them along, or go against them, depending on its direction. It was unbelievable how strong the wind was. Filling the sail as if it were liquid or water, but being entirely invisible.

What Marty was most in awe of, though, was how small he felt. Usually, in Mum's house, he'd feel big. Huge. Like he was too large for the place. The squashiness and the narrowness and the stuffed, packed fullness made him feel like a giant. But out here, he, they . . . they were tiny. And there was something terrifically marvellous about that. They were specks. Flecks on the surface of the water. Nothing but insignificant spots. Nothing for miles and miles around. And you could feel the power of the sea underneath you. The waves moving, cupping the enormous pumpkin as if it were nothing. And there was something freeing about it. It made Marty feel light as a feather. The same feeling he had when he watched Gracie dance.

Gracie was watching him now.

'You know what?' she said. 'I think this is the happiest I've ever seen you.'

Marty smiled. He didn't actually know what to say.

By the middle of the afternoon, Gracie had cracked open one of the flasks of tea, but the waves out in the middle of the sea seemed choppier, so she found pouring it a bit tricky. Marty watched as she tried to tip the tea into the mugs and not burn herself at the same time.

The waves were tipped with white. Ribbons of water cutting the surface of the sea. The pumpkin bobbed about a bit more. Grandad got up and tried to manoeuvre the sail over the biggest waves. Some spray was showering them with salty water every now and again.

'We're OK!' shouted Grandad.

The noise acted differently here too. It was as if the sea breeze snatched it away as it was leaving your mouth. Gracie was listening to the water through the reverberations of the pumpkin. It was like a drum. It hummed, the vibrations circling in its rounded belly.

The engine seemed to be straining in the bumpier conditions. It was whirring a bit too much for Marty's liking.

'Is that going to hold up?' asked Marty.

Grandad looked slightly concerned.

'As long as it gets no worse than this . . .'

Grandad sat down again and looked at his map.

'I reckon we should be seeing land soon . . .'

There was no need to get the binoculars out because, funnily enough, they could tell they were getting nearer to land as the noise started up again. There were more boats, each one's captain giving the pumpkin a double-take. Each one rubbernecking like crazy. Grandad was magnificent, waving back nonchalantly as if sailing a giant pumpkin was the most natural thing in the world. The water calmed as they drew up to a little harbour, and before they knew it they were in France. Actually in France.

Marty jumped ashore and Grandad threw him a rope to moor the pumpkin. Grandad then went to pay the harbour master; after all, all boats have to pay to stay in harbour overnight. It's a bit like a boat B&B. The harbour master was talking on the phone when Grandad knocked on his door. When he looked out of the window, he dropped the handset completely and his mouth fell open. Grandad walked in, put the money on the desk in front of him and left him to it.

They'd brought their sleeping bags, of course, and they had enough food to last them the night. They tucked themselves in and Gracie texted her dad just to say they were OK. Within minutes Grandad was snoring, but Gracie and Marty lay awake for a while, aware of the waves gently slopping against the side of the pumpkin.

'I can't actually believe we made it this far,' said Marty dreamily. 'It just all feels a bit weird.'

'I know,' said Gracie.

She was tired. Tired from the dancing. Tired from the night in the cheap hotel, and the rocking of the water was making her sleepy.

'Goodnight, Marty.' Her eyes were heavy now.

'Goodnight . . .'

CHAPTER TWENTY-NINE

Grandad had woken before Marty and Gracie. He had been to a bakery to get some hot coffee, and by the look of his eyes, which were as big as saucers, it must have been strong. A few children were gathered on the harbour, pointing and giggling, and when Marty appeared with his hair sticking up all over the place they laughed a little more. Grandad set about checking the oil in the engine, and Gracie unfurled herself from the bottom of the boat and stretched out. She yawned as Marty tucked into the croissants that Grandad had bought before pulling her bag towards her and changing the batteries in her processor then replacing it behind her ear.

It was a beautiful morning. The water was calm and

glass-like. There was a softness to the light at this time of year, a certain pink smudginess that Marty liked.

At seven thirty exactly, Grandad fired up the engine and Marty untied the rope. He jumped back into the pumpkin and pushed away from the harbour wall with the broom handle they'd brought with them.

They found the mouth of the Seine easily as the Normandy Bridge humped above it. Marty looked up in awe as they sailed under it and the wonders kept coming after that. There were bridges and grand houses, and they dodged ferries and pleasure boats, each one honking their horns at them in glee. They passed villages and towns whose names Grandad shouted out as they went.

'Caudebec-en-Caux! Rouen! Les Andelys! Vernon! Giverny! That's where Monet's garden is, you know, Marty.'

Marty was struck by their beauty. Gracie and he waved as shoals of cycling children rode past on their way to school. And fishermen shouted out greetings in the morning air. Marty kept his hand on the sail, keeping it in between the riverbanks and trying not to get too near the edges. Gracie stood guard because, since the pumpkin wasn't particularly manoeuvrable, you had to have plenty of warning to get out of the way of things. She sat in the front of the pumpkin keeping guard and shouting out instructions, which Marty and Grandad followed.

As they got nearer Paris, the waterways became busier with tourists and dayboats. Marty looked on in wonder as the riverbanks began to fill up. There were cafes and little stands selling comics and old books. There were artists too, selling their pictures or cartoon portraits to people walking by. And then the city began to come into view.

It was mid-morning by now, and the dawn mists had already been burned off the river by the warm August sun. Marty couldn't help but think that there was something of a mirage about what he saw. It was a dreamscape almost, rising slowly above them.

'Look!' shouted Gracie. 'It's the Arc de Triomphe!'

The river was snaking now, folding back on itself. Showing the city and hiding it at the same time. They rounded another corner and then Marty dropped his compass. It slipped off his knees and on to the floor as he stood up, his mouth agape. Grandad called over to him.

'You all right, Marty?'

Marty nodded silently.

'There it is,' he whispered reverently. 'The Eiffel Tower.'

And there it was, glinting in the morning light. Ancient and brand new at the same time. Its beautiful, curved lines. Its strength.

Gracie looked back at Marty and smiled.

After that, the wonders came thick and fast. The towers of Notre-Dame, the Hôtel de Ville and the Louvre. It felt like being on a film set, but it wasn't. This was real life and they were actually really, really here.

Grandad chugged them into the harbour in the middle of Paris, and Marty did his best to slow the pumpkin down so it wouldn't knock against the harbour wall too hard. He jumped out and tied the pumpkin to a metal hoop embedded into the wall. Grandad switched off the engine and Gracie stood up straight. He couldn't believe it. None of them could believe it. They looked at each other. Speechless.

They were in Paris.

CHAPTER THIRTY

Paris was everything Marty had thought it would be. It was colourful. And fast. It was noisy and full of the most delicious smells he'd ever smelt in his life. And the people looked different, so smart and chic.

The Louvre was a wonder. A pyramidy glassy thing that poked through the ground. And the things that were in there! Artworks and drawings, statues and jewels. Marty spent the whole two hours walking around in gobsmacked silence. He had seen pictures of these things at school. He'd even found a book about art in his mum's house, but to see them in real life was more than he could ever have imagined.

Gracie loved the beautiful statues, their bodies stuck in stone across all time. Graceful. Moving but stock still. She wondered how anyone could make something so cold look so warm and alive. She stood in front of each one and tried to make the same shapes with her body.

Grandad spent his time, thumbs tucked into his waistcoat pockets, shaking his head in wonder.

They had lunch in a cafe on a square. Baguettes with lemonade. And Grandad had some more coffee, which made him bounce with energy. As the day wore on, Marty felt more and more jittery too. They had an ice cream by a beautiful stone fountain, but Marty's stomach was churning, and by the time they sat together for a street artist to draw them on a big piece of paper, he could hardly sit still at all.

By late afternoon, the crowds of eager tourists had started to dissipate, and as the daylight faded Grandad, who had been watching Marty, ruffled his hair.

'Come on, then, son,' he said. 'It's time.'

It was getting late as they made their way to the Eiffel Tower, but that made it even more beautiful as it was all lit up with mellow sparkly lights. Marty gasped when he saw it closer up. It was fantastic. Huge! Beautiful.

Grandad said he'd take the lift, while Gracie and Marty decided to walk.

'You OK?' Gracie asked him.

Marty nodded. He didn't actually have the words to explain how he felt.

'Let's go, then . . .' Gracie smiled and they started their climb.

There were 674 steps to the viewing platform and 1,665 steps to the top. Marty knew that. It was 324 metres tall. Marty knew that too. In fact, he knew everything about it, but being here was an entirely different experience altogether. Gracie was out of breath already and Marty's heart was pounding. Round and round they went, climbing higher and higher. And as they did so more and more of Paris came into view. You could see for miles, the grids of the blocks, the wide avenues. The landscape punctuated every now and again by towers or churches or mosques. Marty knew the mechanics of the place. The tower. He knew how it had been put together, but its sum was somehow more than its parts. It was a beautiful thing. It was magnificent. It was alive . . .

Grandad was waiting for them at the top. He was

looking around in awe, almost as you would in a holy place. The sun was setting behind the city, rimming the dark buildings with gold and orange. Marty drew a sharp breath as he stepped out and saw the view.

He didn't actually know what he'd expected he would feel being here. It had just been a dream. It was like he wanted to be close to something. Find some meaning in something. He stepped forward and Grandad pulled at Gracie's arm to keep her by his side. Marty looked. He closed his eyes a moment and thought about his mum's house; he thought about how much he loved her. He thought about how big the world was. He thought too about how alone he used to feel, but it was funny, because however much he tried to pull up that feeling now he just couldn't do it. He didn't feel alone. He had Grandad and Gracie, and Mum too, although she wasn't with him. He thought he might feel a longing for something else too, but there was nothing. No longing, just a taste for adventure. Marty opened his eyes again and turned and smiled. Grandad and Gracie came to stand either side of him.

'Thanks,' he whispered.

'You're welcome, my boy,' said Grandad, squeezing his hand.

Marty felt Gracie's head rest on his other shoulder.

'You're not disappointed you haven't seen your dad?' Gracie whispered. 'I've been worried about you.'

'No,' Marty answered, looking down at the glittering city. 'He's on his own journey. And who knows? One day maybe our paths will cross, but either way . . .' Marty paused. 'It's OK.'

Grandad held his hand tighter.

'That's my boy,' he said proudly, his voice cracking. 'That's my Marty.'

By the time they made it back to the pumpkin it was really dark. A full moon was throwing down a path across the dark water. They all stepped into the moored boat, and snuggled under the sleeping bags, knowing that they had a long journey home in the morning. They had the harbour to themselves as the whole city seemed to have gone to sleep. Grandad opened a flask of hot chocolate and they ate some cakes they'd picked up from a bakery on the way back and they talked and talked until all three of them were sleepy.

'They call it the City of Lights,' said Grandad.

Gracie smiled.

'What a beautiful name . . .' she said.

'It is, isn't it?' replied Grandad.

The pumpkin rocked gently beneath them as they lay on their backs in the bottom of the boat, and, up above, a million stars were shining with a hundred million possibilities.

CHAPTER THIRTY-ONE

'RIGHTY HO! UP, UP AND AWAY WE GO!'

Marty had never slept more soundly. He had rested properly for the first time in his young life. The rocking and the silence, the breeze and the fresh air had knocked him out completely. Grandad had got up early and walked to a nearby shop for some *pain au chocolat*. They ate in the morning light as all the passing dog walkers gave them very strange looks.

By eleven, they were ready to sail. Grandad had given the engine a quick once-over and they were good to go. Marty untied the rope and threw it into the pumpkin before jumping aboard.

'*AU REVOIR!*' shouted Grandad, laughing. 'Paris, it's been a pleasure!'

Gracie waved too as they started to leave the city behind them. Marty smiled and just whispered a simple 'thanks' under his breath.

The river was much choppier today and the sky was definitely greyer. They had an enormous umbrella to fit on the pumpkin like a teapot lid if it did actually tip it down, but none of them were keen to put that to the test.

The engine seemed to be holding up, but the pattern of the sounds was different today. The waves were rougher, more unpredictable. Marty looked at Grandad with concern.

They were out of the harbour at least, and they all had their life jackets on, but Marty, for some reason, dug out the firework, just in case they needed it. Gracie was quieter today, so was Marty. Now they were on their way home, their spirits were dampened a little. It would be back to school. Back to normality. Back to . . . Marty tried not to think about Mum. Marty noticed that Gracie was looking slightly green around the gills too . . .

'You OK?'

'I'm OK . . . It's a bit rougher today, that's all . . .'

The swell was growing and so was the wind. The

engine was doing practically nothing by now as the sail was billowing and shooting the pumpkin forward. This might have been a good thing, if it wasn't so jerky and choppy. Marty handed Gracie one of the plastic buckets Grandad had brought in case of the pumpkin letting in water. Gracie thanked him. Marty tried to tie everything down, pack everything tight in the bottom of the pumpkin to make sure things didn't sway about. Grandad was working his hardest with the sail. *WHOOSH, CLACK, WHOOSH, CLACK.* The boat would surge forward and then smack down hard on the next lull. *WHOOSH, CLACK.* Grandad looked at the engine with worry, then he sat down and tried to chart where they were. They had another couple of hours at least before reaching Le Havre. Grandad checked over the pumpkin and frowned.

'What's wrong, Grandad?' said Marty.

Grandad was hanging over the side inspecting the outside of the pumpkin.

'It's OK,' his voice came back.

'Should we stop? For a bit?' asked Gracie, trying to ignore her washing-machine stomach. 'Do you think the pumpkin can take it?'

Grandad hauled himself up.

'She'll be fine,' he said, wiping his brow. 'There's a little bit of wear and tear on the outside, but that's all the more reason to keep going, I'd say. We're on a tight schedule if we want to make it back for your mum's birthday and we want this baby to hold up.'

Marty had never missed his mum's birthday. He never had any money for presents, of course. But they'd put some records on the old player and dance around and Marty would be allowed to stay up as late as he liked. The thought of not doing that gave him a sickness in the pit of his stomach that was nothing to do with the swaying pumpkin.

The next hour was horrendous. The swell would lift them up and then drop them, over and over again until they almost didn't know which direction was up and which was down. The towns and cities that they passed on their journey up the Seine whizzed by in a blur as they tried to hang on. Marty had been keeping an eye out for the Normandy Bridge, knowing that one sight of it would mean they were safely back at Le Havre at least, but it was nowhere to be seen.

The wind was blowing roughly, snatching the sail rope out of Marty's hands every now and again, burning his skin as it scratched across his palms. He tried to hold on tight, but his arms were getting tired.

'Let it go!' shouted Grandad eventually. 'The wind's so blustery that there's no point fighting against it.'

'Let it go?' Marty shouted back incredulously.

'Yes! Let it go. We'll just have to drift.'

Marty wasn't sure about this at all, but Grandad seemed to know what he was doing, so Marty just let the rope go. He pulled the sail down and folded it up in a bundle on the floor of the pumpkin. Gracie came to sit down beside him. She'd gone past green now; she was, in fact, almost blue with sickness.

After a while, Grandad came to sit with them.

Marty looked at him in panic. 'What are you doing?'

Grandad smiled. 'You've got to know when to let go sometimes, son.'

Gracie looked across at Marty. 'But there's no one steering . . . ?' she said.

Grandad nodded, and pulled his hat down tighter on his head. 'I know.'

He said this as if it were entirely normal to rush down the Seine in an out-of-control pumpkin.

'You can fight it all you like,' Grandad said, 'but we won't win this one. We've got to just trust we'll be OK.'

Then they spent what seemed like hours bobbing about in the choppy waters, the crumpled sail lying between them.

'Do we need to call anyone?' asked Gracie. 'Are we in trouble?'

Grandad smiled. 'I don't think so.'

By around five in the afternoon, the river had evened out a bit. Grandad had actually taken a snooze and when he awoke he popped his head over the side of the pumpkin to see where they were. Marty looked up at him and watched as a wide grin spread on his face. Then, an almighty darkness rose above them.

'No way!' Marty smiled. 'It's the bridge! We're in Le Havre!'

Grandad smiled too. 'Course we are. It's tidal, you see, the Seine. I always knew we'd end up here . . .'

Grandad winked, and even though Marty wasn't sure

if his grandad was telling the truth or not he grinned back anyway.

That night, they tethered the pumpkin in the harbour and went to buy some food at a little restaurant. They didn't have much money left, but as they were on the last night of their adventure Grandad suggested blowing it all on *moules* with chips and some ice cream.

They ate outside, wrapped up in their coats, watching the dark English Channel ahead of them. Marty laughed as Grandad dipped his bread into his sauce and dribbled it over his chin, and Gracie had double helpings of ice cream since she hadn't been able to eat anything else after all the queasiness. Marty was quieter tonight. Glad that they had got this far and knowing they were on the home straight.

'I've been thinking,' he said carefully. 'I think – I think I know what I want to be.'

Grandad looked up at him and dried his fingers on his trousers. Gracie turned to face him, expectantly. Marty looked down. Embarrassed.

'I think I want to be an architect.'

Grandad studied him in silence. Marty's brow

furrowed now as he focused deep down inside.

'I want to think about how we live. The space we take up in the world. I want to dream things, amazing things that are bigger than us . . . and make them a reality . . .'

Gracie smiled.

'Well,' Grandad said, wiping away a tear, 'I think that's terrific. Absolutely terrific.'

CHAPTER THIRTY-TWO

The drizzle started first thing. Gracie had set her phone alarm for five in the morning. They had four hours of sailing before they got to Southampton. Grandad moaned as he got up and cursed his bad back. Marty sniffed himself. He stank. Not just the normal stinkiness of not washing; he stank of slightly sour pumpkin. The insides of it were now turning slightly slimy and Marty was sure it was sitting a bit lower in the water.

They didn't have any money left for breakfast and since Grandad was sure that they'd be back home around lunchtime, they'd have to hold on until then. Marty looked out to sea as Gracie and Grandad started clearing out the pumpkin. They didn't need anything that was extra weight. There were a few empty petrol canisters and some rubbish that were just taking up space, so Gracie and Grandad walked those to the bin. The sea was so grey today that it was almost impossible to tell where the sea ended and the sky started. Its mood was difficult to read too. Although it wasn't too choppy, it definitely had an undercurrent of something about it.

'We ready?' asked Grandad at last.

Gracie nodded and smiled.

'Let's go home!'

They sailed out of the harbour and bobbed their way in the general direction of Southampton. Marty pulled up the sail today as the wind seemed to be more consistent. He watched as it filled and boosted them forward. They sailed in relative quiet, since there wasn't much traffic around out in the middle of the Channel. Gracie had laid her head on the edge of the pumpkin and was listening through it to the water below. Grandad was talking to the engine in a low voice. Egging it on.

Marty couldn't wait to tell his mum that one of Grandad's schemes had finally worked. That they'd done this absolutely brilliant and ridiculous thing. He imagined opening the door and telling her the whole story. She might not believe him, but that wouldn't stop him. He'd been thinking about her during the night, alone in the house, and he knew that he couldn't make her better. It wasn't his job and it wasn't in his power to do that, but he could live his own life. Make something of himself and maybe in some way show her how brilliant the world could be . . .

Marty was thinking about this when he noticed something. Something that would worry you on dry land, to be fair, but it was even more worrisome when you were in a pumpkin in the middle of a choppy ocean. His socks were wet. He looked down. Wiggled his toes. Yup. They were definitely wet. As Gracie was miles away in her daydreaming, she hadn't noticed.

'Er, Grandad!'

'Hang on, Marty.'

'No, er, Grandad . . .'

'Give me a minute; I need to adjust the engine . . .'

'Er, Grandad, we're taking on water!'

Grandad snapped out of his reverie.

'What?' He looked down. 'Oh no!'

Marty nudged Gracie, nodding towards his wet

feet. She looked up, worried.

'Bucket at the ready!' said Grandad.

There was barely an inch of water in the bottom of the pumpkin, but it was swishing back and forth already. Grandad set about trying to find where it was coming from.

'It's the expanding foam!' he cried. 'The engine has moved. There's a gap!'

The spray from the waves was splashing over them as they SWISH, SWISH, SWISHED from side to side. Marty was feeling sick now too. Weak and sick. He set about trying to scrape up as much of the water as he could, while Grandad tried to steer the boat home as quickly as possible. Gracie concentrated hard on not vomiting violently over everyone.

'We can't be that far out!' cried Grandad.

At first Marty thought he was keeping on top of bailing out the pumpkin, but after a while he felt the water come up to his ankles.

'Grandad! It's no good, Grandad!'

The lady from allotment seven had lent them her binoculars. Grandad had hung them round his neck and every now and again, he'd point them in the direction of what should be the shore and scan to see if he could see land. He tried again. There was nothing.

Gracie had started to help with the water now too, sick or not. This was fast becoming a crisis. She was shovelling water out as fast as she could with the enamel mugs.

Marty was being pushed back and forth now, being knocked from one side of the boat to the other. He and Gracie started a highly complex dance of trying not to knock each other out. As he rocked, his thoughts turned more and more to Mum. He really wanted to see her.

'Can you see land, Grandad? Grandad!'

Grandad was looking, but he couldn't see a thing.

'Just keep trying!' Marty said.

Marty was sure that the boat was sitting much, much lower in the water. The sea seemed to be getting higher around them. He worked faster until the muscles in his arms ached and his stomach was burning. Gracie was white as a sheet by now.

'Marty, are we going to be OK?' she asked.

Marty didn't want to lie to her. This was serious.

'I reckon we should let off that firework, Grandad!'

'I agree!' Grandad shouted over the wind.

Marty couldn't keep himself still long enough to light the match. Every time he got one lit, the wind would blow it out. Every time he got a new one from the box, a spray of water would dampen it.

'Why didn't we bring a lighter?' he shouted in frustration.

Eventually, he jammed the firework into the top of one of the supply bags on the floor of the pumpkin and sat, legs spread to steady himself. Then, his fingers shaking, he managed to scrape a match carefully on the box and guard the flame in his cupped hand to light the firework.

'HEADS DOWN!' he shouted, and Gracie and Grandad ducked.

WHHHHOOOOOOOOOOOOOOOOOOSH!

The rocket vroomed straight up into the air as the boat rocked from side to side and it exploded in an almighty burst of red and orange sparks above them. Then *BOOM!* A secondary explosion, and BOOM! Another! Gracie felt the vibrations in her head and chest and all around her. It was one of the most extraordinary things she had ever experienced.

The pumpkin was still taking on water, faster than before, and the lip of the pumpkin was now only a few centimetres above the surface of the sea. This wasn't good at all.

'I'm so tired!' cried Gracie.

'We've got to keep going!' gasped Marty, grabbing the bucket again. 'We've got to be nearly there!'

Grandad stood up again, and steadied his wobbly self.

He squinted into the binoculars and Marty watched his face as it suddenly broke into a smile.

'Can you see anything yet?'

Grandad's belly started jiggling up and down with a rounded giggle.

Gracie looked at Marty.

'What is it, Grandad?'

His giggle turned into a belly laugh.

Marty tugged at his jacket.

'Grandad, can you see land?'

Grandad took off the binoculars and gave them to Marty.

'Have a look yourself, boy . . .'

Marty squished the lenses against his eyes and stood up. He tried to keep his balance. Squinted. Sea. Sea. More sea. Until . . . He gasped. There was the shore. In the far, far distance, but . . . coming towards them were boats. Big ones. Small ones. Fishing ones. Hobby ones. And everyone was waving flags. It was incredible! Marty started laughing too.

'There are boats! Loads of them! Fishermen! Lifeguards! They're coming to meet us!' cried Marty.

Gracie smiled.

It seemed to take forever, but eventually they found themselves encircled by boats. There were signs painted with the words WELCOME HOME, and flags and bunting. There were cheers and laughter. There were film crews crammed on to boats, and flying drones filming all the action. Grandad tried to keep the pumpkin steady in order to stop them tipping over with all the excitement and the extra movement in the water.

They were getting nearer and nearer the harbour, and, slowly and steadily, Marty and Gracie and Grandad chugged their way in. There were schoolchildren lined up along every inch of the harbour walls and a man with a golden chain round his neck, who Marty presumed was the town mayor, waiting for them at the dock. Marty had never felt so speechless.

'Welcome home, Marty and Gracie and Grandad!' the crowd cried.

Gracie stood up as Grandad threw a rope on to the harbourside so they could tie the pumpkin up safely. Then Marty saw something more wondrous than anything he had seen so far. On the quayside, looking small and nervous, was his mum. That man, the one he'd seen in the house, was standing by her side. Marty stared in disbelief. She locked her eyes on to his face. Marty jumped out of the boat and ran and ran; she rushed to meet him halfway down the slipway. They hugged. Tight. Held each other as people cheered. His mum held his face and stared into it.

'I'm so proud of you! I'm so, SO proud of you!' She had tears in her eyes.

'What are you doing here?' he gasped, out of breath with excitement and joy and disbelief.

She looked back towards the man, who waved down at Marty.

'That man over there . . . He's called Neil. He's my counsellor . . .'

'Counsellor?' asked Marty.

'He's been helping me . . .'

Everything seemed to fall into place.

'I need to sort out what's in here –' she tapped her head with her finger – 'so I can sort out what's in the house . . . but you – you are such a good example to me . . .'

Marty buried his head in her shoulder and they held each other for a very long time.

CHAPTER THIRTY-THREE

Colin the milkman had come to pick them up with a rented van since he'd drowned the milk float. As victory parades go, it wasn't the most glamorous thing you've ever seen. Not like those when footballers crawl through town on the top of a luxury bus, but Marty thought it was perfect. Most of the spectators had gone home now, everyone grinning. But for everyone else there was a lot more celebrating to do. Grandad and Mum had shared a quiet moment and Gracie was sitting with her dad. He'd wrapped a blanket around her and they were talking animatedly. Marty looked over and smiled.

'Your mum gone home?' asked Grandad.

Marty nodded.

'What she did, the way she came out here, took guts.

A lot of strength.' Marty knew that. 'She's absolutely brilliant,' said Grandad, 'and one day she may even realize that herself.'

Colin was waiting for them and it was starting to get dark.

'So,' said Marty as he looked at the pumpkin, which was glowing bright in the last light of day, 'what are we going to do with her, then?'

Grandad put his arm around him. He waved over one of the fishermen and whispered in his ear. The fisherman nodded and climbed down the steps into the harbour. Gracie's dad came towards them and shook Grandad's hand.

'Thanks for looking after Gracie.'

Grandad smiled. 'She doesn't need much looking after, but you're welcome anyway.'

'I was thinking,' he said. 'Gracie says you're the best gardener she's ever seen . . .'

Marty was sure he saw Grandad blush a little.

'Oh, I don't know about that,' he stuttered.

'It's just that I know you and I got off on the wrong foot, but I'd love to learn a little more. I've never had time, really, but I've been thinking that maybe I've been working too hard.'

Grandad beamed.

'Well, I could always do with a hand and, I tell you, the fresh air does you wonders.'

Gracie had sidled up to them now just in time to hear the little fisherman's tugboat honk his horn. They all looked across the water. The fisherman had taken the guy rope and pulled the pumpkin out to sea. Grandad put up his hand and signalled to the fisherman to let her go. As the sun sank over the horizon, they watched the pumpkin slip slowly under the water. Marty looked up as Grandad wiped a tear from his eye.

'That's where she belongs –' Grandad's voice was almost breaking – 'in the realms of dreams.'

Marty reached out and squeezed his hand.

'Well done, Grandad.'

CHAPTER THIRTY-FOUR

The party had been going for *hours*! Everyone had made their way back to the allotments, and trestle tables had been filled with food from the four corners of the world. After all, it was harvest time, and there was an abundance of fruits and veg everywhere. Grandad had given several interviews and everyone had been laughing and dancing all over the allotments. There would be so many stories in tomorrow's papers and everyone would know what they had done.

Marty was sitting, exhausted but happy, by the fire when Gracie came to join him.

'I got in . . .' she said.

'I knew you would.' Marty smiled.

'They phoned today. Left a message.'

Marty thought about what this meant for his friend for a moment.

'Dad phoned Mum; they're both really happy for me.'

Marty smiled.

'I'm really proud of you,' said Marty, and he really, truly meant it.

'Ditto,' she said. 'You do realize that even if I have to stay at the school in the week, I'm going to be here every weekend.'

'I know,' Marty said. 'And, anyway, to spend the week

apart won't be a bad thing because, to be honest, you're starting to get on my nerves.'

They grinned at each other.

'And I think,' said Gracie, 'after all this coverage in the papers, you're going to be quite the hero in school on Monday. You wouldn't have time for me anyway, not with all your fans wanting to talk to you . . .'

The last of the stragglers were starting to make their way home now and the sky was getting a bit lighter with the first whisperings of dawn.

Marty was sure he had recognized one of the figures dancing in the darkness, but he just couldn't put a finger on who it was . . . And then he appeared right in front of Marty.

It was Mr Garraway! In a kilt!

Marty jumped up.

'Hello, sonny.' Mr Garraway smiled.

'You're looking very smart, sir,' Marty said.

'Well, it's a celebration, isn't it? Your trip was absolutely brilliant, Marty.'

Marty grinned. 'Thanks, sir.'

A woman Marty didn't know came over and wrapped

her arm round Mr Garraway's waist.

'I wanted to tell you that I've got a new job, Marty.'

Marty's face fell. 'You're leaving the school?' he asked.

Mr Garraway shook his head. 'No, sonny. I'm your new head teacher!'

Marty looked back at Gracie in disbelief.

'The big bad wolf is retiring . . .' He winked. Then he suddenly looked serious. 'Oh God, she's not behind me, is she?'

Marty shook his head and laughed.

'It's what I wished for when I came to see your pumpkin.'

'That's amazing, sir!'

'It is, isn't it? Aye, right.' He looked at the woman next to him. 'We'd better go. I just wanted to say thanks.'

Marty nodded. 'It's OK.'

Mr Garraway was about to turn when he looked back at Marty again.

'Oh, and did you give any thought to your choices? What you want to do?'

Marty smiled. 'Yes. Yes, I did, actually.'

'Good,' Mr Garraway said. 'Good. Well, I'll see you on Monday.'

Marty sat down again next to Gracie as Grandad approached.

'*WHOOOF,*' said Grandad as he sat down too, exhausted. He'd been dancing for hours.

Grandad had been handing out a seed to everyone as they left the party. Pressing it into their palms as if he were giving them the most precious gift in the world. And, in some ways, he was. He was giving them a seed to grow. Some hope. A little seed that could contain anything they wanted to imagine.

'I've had a wonderful time,' Grandad said, his voice deep and content.

'So have I,' said Gracie.

'Me too,' said Marty.

'But do you know what?' Grandad added.

Marty and Gracie were looking into the dying flames of the fire as a new morning woke around them. Grandad hesitated a moment, making sure he had Gracie's and Marty's full attention.

'I've always kind of fancied flying . . . How much do you think a giant marrow would weigh?'

Gracie and Marty looked at each other in disbelief.

Grandad was tapping his chin with his finger, deep in thought.

'I wonder if we could fit some wings on one . . . ?'

This is a list of what Grandad has:

687,987,679,090 giant pumpkin seeds
(those things have a LOT of seeds inside)
1 grandson who loves him very much
1 daughter who comes to drink tea
with him sometimes
Lots of ideas

This is a list of what Marty has:

One grandad who loves him very much
1 mum who laughs a bit these days and is working
hard at recovery for both their sakes
1 dancer best friend
Lots of ideas

And you know what?
This is enough.

ABOUT THE AUTHOR

Caryl Lewis is a multi-award-winning Welsh novelist, children's writer, playwright and screenwriter. Her breakthrough novel *Martha, Jac a Sianco* (2004) is widely regarded as a modern classic of Welsh literature. It is on the Welsh curriculum, and the film adaptation – with a screenplay by Lewis herself – went on to win six Welsh BAFTAS and the Spirit of the Festival Award at the 2010 Celtic Media Festival. Lewis's other screenwriting work includes BBC/S4C thrillers *Hinterland* and *Hidden*. Lewis is a visiting lecturer in Creative Writing at Cardiff University, and lives with her family on a farm near Aberystwyth.

ABOUT THE ILLUSTRATOR

George Ermos is an illustrator, maker and avid reader from England. He works digitally and loves illustrating all things curious and mysterious. He is always trying to incorporate new artiness from the various world cultures he reads about and explores.